WARRIOR OF LOVE

ANDREW MEYRICK

First Edition - 2012
Second Edition - October 2015

Copyright © Andrew Meyrick 2015
You can reach Andrew & Elo via email at: andrew@warriorsoflove.net

All rights reserved. No part of this publication may be reproduced, stored in a retrieval system, or transmitted in any form or by any means, electronic, mechanical, photo-copying or otherwise, without the prior written consent of the publisher. Short extracts may be used for review purposes.

Unless otherwise indicated, all Scripture quotations are taken from The New International Version. Copyright © 1973, 1978, 1984 by International Bible Society® Used by permission. All rights reserved worldwide.

Scripture quotations marked AMP are from the Amplified Bible. Old Testament copyright © 1965, 1987 by the Zondervan Corporaation. The Amplified New Testament copyright © 1954, 1958, 1987 by the Lockman Foundation. Used by permission.

Scripture quotations marked NKJV are taken from The New King James Bible. Copyright © 1979, 1980, 1982, by Thomas Nelson, Inc., publishers. Used by permission.

Scripture quotations marked NASB are taken from The New American Standard Bible. Copyright © 1960, 1962, 1963, 1968, 1971, 1972, 1973, 1975, 1977, 1995 by The Lockman Foundation

Scripture quotations marked KJV are taken from the Holy Bible, King James Version, Cambridge, 1769.

ISBN 978-1-729753-31-6
Printed in the United Kingdom

www.freedompublishing.org

Contents

Endorsements	5
In Other's Words	9
Acknowledgements	11
Foreword	13
Introduction	17
Paradise Lost	27
Paradise Regained	37
Why Enter God's Army	41
Basic Qualifications	51
The Opposition	55
Bootcamp	61
Regular Army	77
The Front Line	85
Special Forces	95
Lessons Learnt & Experiences	105
Body, Soul & Spirit	125
Our Amazing Story	143
Postscript	149
Toolbox	159
Warrior's Quiver	175
Booklist	181
End Notes	183

ENDORSEMENTS

Warriors of Love is a cornucopia. Andrew brings forth the heart of the Father and its interweaving with the heart of His children. Andrew and Elo carry the DNA of heaven's love in a radiant way. In this work, the spring of love comes flowing beautifully. I have watched Andrew direct the gentle arrow of the Lord's love with such effectiveness. That gift of being an unhindered conduit of divine love comes out very clearly. I recommend this book to any who desire to be a warrior of God's love

Dr Adonijah O Ogbonnaya
USA

In Warriors of Love, Andrew presents the Christian life as it should be, simpler than we think, yet more profound and powerful than we could ever imagine. Through his personal writing style Andrew takes us on a journey of making it easy to apprehend more of the Kingdom. This book will further equip all who venture into its pages and I recommend you do just that!

Joaquin Evans
Former Director, Bethel Healing Rooms
Bethel Activation Teams, USA

Andrew Meyrick is a man in passionate pursuit to know intimately and completely the heart of God. In his book Andrew shares openly the very real journey he is on, releasing to us the keys and treasures that have become a part of him as he encounters the love and ways of the King and the realm of His Kingdom. Andrew has provided a way for each of us wherever we are at in our walk with God to go deeper and higher. He provides a language that helps us to see more clearly who Jesus is, and who we are in Him. Insight is gained into who we are becoming as we are fashioned and formed into the likeness of Jesus. Andrew gives us a taste of the incredible relationship available to us as we say 'yes' to God's invitation to belong to Him. The content, as you will experience, is the testimony of Jesus written on the heart of a man who has given his life to know Him.

Rev. Liz Wright
The Bridal Company, UK

This book is a must read!! Andrew has written a book that will inspire and activate the readers to be challenged to become present day warriors who ultimately will become heroes. They will become the new breed that was born to establish and increase the Kingdom of God!!

Wendell McGowan
Wendell McGowan Ministries/Prophetic Revivalist

I have known Andrew as an active member of our church here in London for the past eighteen months. He has a real heart to see the body of Christ mobilised and equipped to heal Nations. I pray that this book blesses you and encourages you to believe for an open heaven over your life, and that you will fulfill the plans and dreams the Lord has placed in your heart.
[Isaiah 60:1-7]
Pastor Ian McCormack
Kings Gate Church - London UK

ENDORSEMENTS

Andrew Meyrick is one of a new generation of radical believers God is raising up. His book 'Warriors of Love' highlights the steps one man has taken on his journey from living an 'ordinary' life to believing and seeing the impossible in double quick time! It is full of little gems and resources and there are many to search out as you read it. I am very happy to commend it to you.

Andrew Leakey
In:Courage, Bath UK

IN OTHER'S WORDS

I recommend shutting yourself in the secret closet with this one. It is definitely not a casual read. Some chapters are meatier than others and will require time to chew. The Holy Spirit confirmed some of its message to me by other means too, and lies that I had believed for years were exposed quite effortlessly. Moreover, as the book progresses, the enemy is actually forced to manifest out of hiding and into His wonderful light. The authority of the Lord through its pages is evident and even contagious. The oversight displayed by Andrew brings hope time and time again as one's lifelong mysteries are revealed and the common humanity in life's seasons is laid bare... And the only fit response by the reader is to burst out in worship of Him who counselled the birth of Warriors of Love. Andrew wisely draws on the natural and spiritual, side by side, that we may understand of the end-time army and of our place in it. There is a very helpful expounding of redemptive gifts and gifting types, leading to individual confirmation and commission by the Holy Spirit. Without forgetting the abundance of scriptural treasures forming the bulk of the truth, so powerful in this book. The overall flavour of this uncommon read being encouragement, love, kindness and grace - I am considering bulk buying for the church's Prophetic Intercessors Group I am part of as a Christmas blessing!
Stella B

Excellent Foundation and reference book. Would recommend every Christian read this. Great truths for new Christians and as a refresher for those who've been a Christian longer. Inspiring testimonies and an encouraging read. Loved it! Thank you Andrew.
Linda T

This easy read is a summary of Andrew Meyricks journey with Jesus.... and it is an interesting one. It is not deep in explanation but the pithy summaries of God encounters, with lightning quick life applications, take this from simple testimony status into a work that will enable the reader to genuinely encounter Jesus for themselves.
Steve J

This is a must for every Christian as you will read life and power into your soul and spirit! Love the way it is written and will leave a lasting impression of Andrew's unique insight into our Papa's heart for total freedom for us and leading the way and path for others. Read it, be challenged and others will read it again and again..! Love is the answer...HIS LOVE...Be blessed and strengthened by reading this book!
Annette B

I remember seeing you on Naomi Ketcher's Facebook page, and seeing your book came out, I ordered it. It made it's way to my nightstand last week and after a powerful weekend hearing from Bobby Conner, James Maloney and Bob Jones, God said NOW! I have only read the introduction and chapter one and could hardly put it down. When I went to sleep I could feel the frequency of heaven vibrating though my spirit! Thank you for your obedience and willingness to hear Papa on this book. Looking forward to reading and rereading.
Lisa

I have enjoyed this amazing book. Full of revelation and love. Easy to read and digest over and over again. A must read. Freckles

ACKNOWLEDGEMENTS

'The world would use us just as it did the martyrs if we loved God as they did.' Bishop Wilson[1]

There are so many people that have contributed to helping me get to where I am today.

In my 'unsaved' state although 'believing' in God and Jesus, the examples and counsel and teaching by Dom Edward Corbould OSB and Cardinal Basil Hume have shown me what humility is about and the path that I should have followed initially. For a long time I felt the only way one led a life dedicated to the Lord was through being in a monastery or as an ordained priest.

I had not understood there was another way that allowed me to operate in the secular world as a priest and minister. This way was all about having a personal relationship with my Maker. I did not need intermediaries to gain access to the Throne. I was a minister and priest by Heavenly Royal appointment.

Liturgy, canons, regulations, observances and protocol all clouded the main issue. Getting to know God intimately was what mattered, and doing His will, not mine.

I owe much to my great friend Elise Woodrow who became my spiritual counsellor in 2000. She led me to the Lord in an unequivocal way. More later.

Kris Mikkerson, Tim Segedin, Pete Wilson and Gary Clarke from Hillsong Church London for shepherding me.

More recently, I owe much to the following Revivalists for their inspiration, guidance and encouragement: Bobby Conner, Gary Oates, Bill Johnson, Danny Silk, Kris Vallotton, Chad Dedmon, Jerame Nelson, Joaquin Evans, Bishop Adonijah Ogbonnaya my apostolic mentor and Os Hillman

Thanks to Pastor Ian McCormack and his wife Jane for their protection and counsel and love.

Thanks to Pastors Hugo and Hanneke Van Driel of Yapton Free Church for their fiery love of the Holy Spirit and support, love and guidance.

Thanks to Dom Muir for being such a fiery inspiration and a warrior for the Lord. He has been a good and loyal friend. His zeal and tireless energy in evangelism through his street ministry and mission NowBelieve as well as his encouragement has kicked me out of my chrysalis into full flight, never to return.

Thanks to Jonathan Cavan, a close friend and brother who resonates so strongly with me in the Spirit and has pushed me forward.

Thanks to Lulu and Liz and the Guildford Prayer School princesses for unlocking scrolls and imparting the Seven Spirits of God. Guildford has been a key time of commissioning and discovery of His purpose and destiny for me.

Thanks to my brother Brian Trueman who has taught me the Father's love and is a true brother I never had.

I thank my Lord and Maker for all the love He has poured in to me. My purpose in life is to please Him only.

Thanks to my warrior friends and brothers and sisters in Christ who have catapulted me into coming forward and being so supportive; Elise, Jean Claude, Miriam, Nomes, Julia, Miranda, Joseph, Jonathan, Helena, Brian, Adam, Naomi B2, JJ, Scott, Lulu and her princesses, Tracy, Brenda, Sue G, Catherine, Peter G, Krisztina, Andrea B, Diana, Pete and Lindsay, Bea and Dave, Pip and Sophie, Ruthann, Roz, Corinna, Tim, Wes, Zoe, Andrew L, Kim, Ellie, Chrissie, Debs, Ceri, Juanita, Stuart, Emmy, Mark, Steve B, Giles and Sheila, Anne F, Paul and Madeleine G, Jennifer S, Nigel and Jane, Jen O,

ACKNOWLEDGEMENTS

Helen B, Hugh and Ginny C, Rollo, Roy, Ian D. Jules S., Steven A for guiding me on publishing. And all those who have escaped my memory!

My thanks especially to my dear friend David Powell who picked up the gargantuan task of taking Warriors of Love from a self published amateur publication to becoming a thoroughly professional second edition. His spiritual resonance and insight, coupled with his imaginative vision and rigorous biblical review, makes me a very proud and grateful author. He is now getting Warrior's Quiver in to the same shape.

Special thanks to Brian, Julia, Ellie and Diana for proof reading and my beloved wife Elo Ania for her additions and editing.

Thanks to Ian Clayton and Mike Parsons for allowing me to insert their diagram.

Special gratitude to my wife Elo Ania who has guided and helped editing this edition, writing our story and adding all the scriptural references in the end notes. A true labour of love, guided by the Holy Spirit.

Thanks to my daughters Gemma, Jessica and Maddie, and their mother Ali who have lovingly put up with the ways that I have changed, hopefully for the better.

Thanks and love to my mother Sue for her generous help in publishing the book.

Endnotes
[1] Thomas Wilson (20 December 1663–7 March 1755) was Anglican Bishop of Sodor and Man between 1697 and 1755

Foreword

USA In this unique Kairos moment, we are hearing a clarion call for the long-awaited army of God to rise up throughout the earth in power. "Warriors of Love" is
by far the most compelling book I have ever read when it comes to defining the training process and all that it takes to be qualified and approved to serve in God's army.

Every army that rises to greatness, first has to train and equip its soldier's to be highly skilled before they can ever enter the battlefield. In order for soldiers to be the most effective they can be, they undergo intense training at boot-camp, where they learn the "basics". God's army is no different.

Everyone who joins, enlists out of passionate love for their King. A true warrior for Christ joins out of great conviction and is willing to endure whatever it takes to make it through the arduous process of refinement to ultimately operate at their fullest potential. Truly this is one of the most comprehensive training guides in our time.

"Warriors of Love" will deeply impact and transform you from beginning to end. Whether you have already been walking at a high level of maturity or having just received Jesus into your heart as a born again believer, you will find a treasure trove of wisdom and understanding gleaned through Andrew Meyrick's own remarkable journey.

Page by page, you will feel as though you are listening to Andrew himself, sharing deep truths and laying out a blueprint for consistency in Christ, so that you run for the prize in Him and ultimately win it. "Warriors of Love" was birthed out of his own experiential walk with Christ, having been raised as an orphan and enduring many seasons of brokenness that ultimately turned into victories. I have had the joy of knowing Andrew for years and I can attest to the great measure of the character and spiritual fruit I see that manifests daily in the lives he touches around the world.

Andrew is a walking celebration of Christ and the victory Jesus attained for us on the Cross. He revels in the truth; he is passionate for the deep things of God and he fosters an environment of sound character with an unwavering moral compass. Andrew has a shepherd's heart and he models what strong and wise leadership should look like. There is a deep river of wisdom that flows through his life and wherever it touches, lives are transformed.

"Warriors of Love" is a practical survival guide to help you understand how to maneuver on the battlefield with courage, skill and honor. Our greatest call is walking in our true Kingdom character which mandates a consistency in every aspect of our lives. Our gaze is always fixed on the King and magnifying His name in all we do, so that others can clearly see Him.

This book is absolutely refreshing beyond every expectation and I believe it will go down as one of the classics in modern literature. There are times you will find yourself lingering in passages as the Holy Spirit is expanding His presence within you. If you long in any way for the true depths and riches in Christ, you will consume this treasure and refer to it often throughout your walk. "Warriors of Love" has the power to dramatically change countless lives and I believe it is one that you'll highly recommend to others and also give out as a cherished gift many times over.

Gary Beaton
Transformation Glory Ministries

Introduction

'The knowledge of God is very far from the love of Him.' Pascal

This is a story of redemption of one ordinary person and his journey. Of Paradise lost and then regained.

This is a handbook for everyone. It is a book to encourage anyone who feels they have been robbed of justice during their life, especially if aspirations and dreams have been curtailed.

Your Creator God has always intended that you fulfil the destiny He has planned for you. Any block or impediment hindering this has come from a very different source.[1]

WHY IS THIS BOOK CALLED WARRIORS OF LOVE?

All the way through the Bible, the men and women that God chose were ordinary humble people that turned into warriors: Gideon, David, Elijah, Joseph, Jonah, Nehemiah, Ruth, Esther, Peter, James, John, Andrew, etc.

What is a warrior? 'A brave or experienced soldier or fighter.'

Why love? Love is all that is needed. It conquers everything.[2] God is Love![3]

All the weaponry below is rooted in Love:[4]

Praise.

The Word of God.

The Blood of Jesus.

Prayer.

The power of testimony.

The power of the Holy Spirit and His gifts.

The Name of Jesus.

Fasting. [e.g saying 'No' to things that are not good for us]

For the weapons of our warfare are not carnal but mighty in God for pulling down strongholds, casting down arguments and every high thing that exalts itself against the knowledge of God, bringing every thought into captivity to the obedience of Christ. 2 Corinthians 10:4-5

Warriors of Love is a book to exalt the King of Kings and Lord of Lords: Jesus Christ.[5] As someone said, we are His Noble Subjects. None of us is ordinary. We are all part of a Royal Family.[6]

Our only purpose is to exalt Him or lift Him up. He created us for His enjoyment and purpose.[7] Like the little boy in the film Toy Story, all He wants to do is to cuddle us, cherish us and have fun with us, and see us grow in His knowledge and our destiny. He wants us to burn for Him in the 'burning in Love sense'.

Although I talk about events, supernatural signs, wonders and healings through the book, please forgive me where I do not succeed in downplaying my role in these events and celebrate the process of how God's master plan rolls out.

It is not about us. It is all about Him.

Just as Jesus chose for His followers a bunch of misfits, including me, He continues to look to the lost, the meek, the sick, the fallen, the addicted and the controlled to break from their shackles and come to serve Him.[8] This is the army He is building now to take back what has been lost from the beginning of the world.

Why do ex-cons have such power in the Word of God when they are restored? Or why are healed people so fired up when they overcome grave terminal illnesses? It is simple. They have tasted the incredible forgiving and loving uncreated God.[9] Where they had no faith, now there is an abundance of hope and confidence IN Him.[10]

God's army is made up of previously weak humans who have been restored through faith and healed supernaturally through His goodness.[11] Some will remain as 'work in progress' for a while.

Jesus had little patience for the religious and self-satisfied who talked godliness but did not practice it.

His venom for the legalists was strongly contrasted with His softness and love for the underdog.

Even now, he has little truck for the whingers and moaners who speak behind people's backs or spend their time correcting people.[12]

Peter, Jesus' right hand man was weak of faith. He was a 'motor mouth.' He was an extrovert who often rushed into things. He had all the potential leadership skills of a gang leader: cocky and full of bravado.

James and John, the 'sons of thunder,' were always trying to be at the top of the pile, but showed little humility.

Judas was a conniving moneyman whom Jesus put in charge of funds knowing full well he would be tempted.

Thomas, after so many miracles and time with Christ would not believe his friends had seen the risen Christ unless he put his hands into Christ's wounds. He was given that opportunity a week later. His utter remorse and repentance was touching as he fell to the floor when Jesus presented himself.

'My Lord and My God' he said. Then Jesus told him, "Because you have seen me, you have believed; blessed are those who have not seen and yet have believed." John 20:29

We are indeed blessed!

So do not think you have to be squeaky clean. It helps, but you can be in transit to the perfection He requires.[13]

It is difficult to have a spliff in your hand and proselytise to a coke addict that he should give up drugs.

How can one persuade a girl to give up being a prostitute if you cannot honour women and your wife as you have one night stands abroad?[14]

How do you reconcile getting an alcoholic to stop killing himself or herself when you have a double whiskey in your hand?

How can you lecture on peace, love and forgiveness if when you get home you terrorise your children with conditional love?

People do of course act out these counterfeit dual roles, but the Lord sees all.

How long do you lecture moral probity and integrity and Christian values as a politician when you are cheating the taxman or not declaring honestly in Parliament or Congress? God catches up with you in the end.

It is difficult to be a good policeman or lawmaker and uphold the law when you are physically abusing your wife at home.

A powerful businessman who is a scion of leadership in industry, yet when at home allows himself to be bullied by his wife. It happens.

Is not your view on life or your impact going to be skewed by these issues when you try to help others? Are not your motives bigoted?[15]

I owe a lot to Pastor George Ndichu at Diani Church, Mombassa, Kenya who spoke over me on Sunday 22 August 2011. I had been invited to preach at his church with a colleague, Peter Garbett. Before I spoke, he declared prophetic words from the Lord over me, which included a statement that I would return to Kenya but not before I had written the book, which I would come back with, for them. My jaw dropped as I hoisted in the message. At the end of the service I needed to have a chat with him. The Lord would give me the title and contents. I had created a group on Facebook that the Lord had titled 'Warriors of Love'. It was by 'invitation only' though people could apply to be a part of it. The object was to bring together like-minded hungry people who put their Lord and Saviour first in everything they did. I quickly realised that Warriors of Love had to be the title of the book I was about to write.

The week in Kenya on a Now Believe mission trip was life changing for me in so many ways. It showed me how love conquers all through our actions, words and behaviours.

It had driven home the verse Ephesians 6:12:

INTRODUCTION

For our struggle is not against flesh and blood, but against the rulers, against the authorities, against the powers of this dark world and against the spiritual forces of evil in the heavenly realms.

Our mission involved conducting a 'warfare of love' on people.

The enemy (satan) came to kill, steal and destroy.

Jesus however, came to give back life, restore and recreate.[16]

The mission to Kenya cemented my love of the African people, especially the younger generation. It confirmed to me God's love for the hungry, sick, lonely and lost. It had shown how, by contrast, the UK and the USA were deeply ingrained in unbelief, complacency, bigotry and hedonism. It showed even more clearly the power of prayer, which in its most basic form is fervently talking with God. The trip to Kenya also showed me the stark contrast between true freedom, and captivity its antithesis.

On returning to London I prayed and soaked and one early morning, the name 'Erasmus' was put on my mind. Suddenly I saw the Latin title: 'Enchiridion Militis Christiani - A handbook of a Christian knight'. This was a book that Desiderius Erasmus had written for a friend who knew of a soldier needing advice. It was a book on how to 'walk the walk' rather than just 'talk the talk' regarding Christian lifestyle. Less observance of rites, more about being Christ-like as a lifestyle.

It became clear that the Lord wanted this to be an update on the book, and also a manual/handbook based on some of my experiences and applied wisdom that He had graciously given me.

I have always had a love of the paintings and engravings of Albrecht Durer. Durer and Erasmus knew each other and one of the most enduring engravings today is that of one of Erasmus by Durer in his study writing. However I chose an illustration from 'the Knight Death and the Devil' as although not commissioned, it is believed the painter produced the engraving to honour Erasmus's book the Enchiridion.

The following is an excerpt from Heilbrun Timeline of Art History:

> 'Dürer's Knight, Death, and the Devil is one of three large prints of 1513-14 known as his Meisterstiche (master engravings). The other two are Melancholia I and Saint Jerome in His Study. Though

not a trilogy in the strict sense, the prints are closely interrelated and complementary, corresponding to the three kinds of virtue in medieval scholasticism - theological, intellectual, and moral. Called simply the Reuter (Rider) by Dürer, Knight, Death, and the Devil embodies the state of moral virtue. The artist may have based his depiction of the "Christian Knight" on an address from Erasmus's Instructions for the Christian Soldier (Enchiridion militis Christiani), published in 1504: "In order that you may not be deterred from the path of virtue because it seems rough and dreary... and because you must constantly fight three unfair enemies - the flesh, the devil, and the world - this third rule shall be proposed to you: all of those spo-

oks and phantoms which come upon you as if you were in the very gorges of Hades must be deemed for naught after the example of Virgil's Aeneas... Look not behind thee." Riding steadfastly through a dark Nordic gorge, Dürer's knight rides past Death on a Pale Horse, who holds out an hourglass as a reminder of life's brevity, and is followed closely behind by a pig-snouted Devil. As the embodiment of moral virtue, the rider modeled on the tradition of heroic equestrian portraits with which Dürer was familiar from Italy is undistracted and true to his mission. A haunting expression of the vita activa, or active life, the print is a testament to the way in which Dürer's thought and technique coalesced brilliantly in the "master engravings."'

INTRODUCTION

So there we are, The Warriors of Love. 'Love conquers all' as we are told. Love is the ultimate weapon.'

It is ironic that this phrase was quoted by Virgil a Roman who was not a Christian or Jew and died nineteen years before the birth of Christ. I like to think he was a forerunner of John the Baptist heralding the King of King's arrival, the Man who embodied and is the visible image of the Invisible God.[18]

This book is intended to be a manual for the aspiring 'end-time soldier', taking him or her from boot camp through to fully-fledged 'front line warrior'.

This book is addressed to the weak, the fallen, the lost, the downhearted, reformed, unreformed and overtly unhappy. It is especially addressed to those who feel injustice has been done to them, to those who are angry with people and life. It is also for those 'sitting on the fence.' It is definitely addressed to the smug, the self-satisfied, the over-confident, the materially successful and the superficially happy, who often wear masks to hide deep hurts. It is addressed to the spiritually blind and to those who live in the Word only but not the Spirit, or vice versa.

Many will be incredulous that it will be possible to join this army. Many more experienced who read this will be using it as an aide-memoir to remind them what to do when the pressures are on. When they need to go back to basics. What fundamentals have they forgotten?

Not all will want to be front line.

Some will be very happy to be chosen to support.

Some will be the strategists in communication.

Some will provide air cover through intercession and prayer.

Some will be in the trauma and battlefield hospitals healing the wounded and sick through the Lord.

Others will want to be trailblazers, scouts, and intelligence gatherers behind enemy lines.

Many will be prepared to be in the front line and utterly ready to lay down their lives at any point.

This book is intended for all.

It will 'spook' some people initially as they come to grips with the power of the Almighty, Lord of Lords and King of Kings. It will teach them a healthy reverential fear of the Lord.[19] It will teach them of the necessity to get over fear of man as quickly as possible.[20]

The Lord spoke to me one day, saying, "How will anyone get round to having a reverential fear of Me if they have fear of man, as they are putting man above Me?"

I receive not glory from men [I crave no human honour, I look for no mortal fame] John 5:41 AMP

If we do not look for approval and admiration in the first place, we are not going to miss it if we do not get it! If we are searching and needy, when we do not get approval, we feel lost, down and rejected. This is fear of man. Flush it! You never needed it. The Godhead adores you and loves everything you do for them. Why do you need any other approval?[21] It is vanity, pride, selfishness and insecurity on your part.

As Adlai Stevenson said: 'Flattery is all very well as long as you don't inhale!'

This is a book about joining a different kind of army than that of the norm.

The war between 'good and evil' has been won, but skirmishes continue to rage by a losing enemy desperate to take as many souls with him before he is devoured. He is an enemy, with little chance of forgiveness or reconciliation.

One Army is free and unfettered.[22] The other is captive living under fear and pain.[23]

Which one will you join?

The ordinance and the weaponry are different. The firepower is awesome and dangerous to handle. Only with obedience, care and loving tenderness can it be used.[24]

The people we fight alongside are different. Colour, age, ethnicity, church, social background and financial situation have no relevance.[25]

One criteria common to all is that fully-fledged Warriors are prepared to lay their earthly lives down for their Saviour Jesus Christ.[26] Why? Well, they are going to Heaven anyway. This life on earth is but a miniscule strand of Eternity.

Warriors will already have gone through the baptism of dying to death and being restored to eternal life.[27] By His stripes they are healed and by His cross and resurrection they have salvation and eternity to look forward to.[28] They also have the privilege of bringing Heaven to Earth every day whenever they want to. They have the honour of hosting His Presence!

Friendships in the Kingdom are quickly acquired and everlasting.[29] There is total trust, honour, respect and love.

Warriors believe in angels, that they are there to help us at all times, under request only from the Lord.[30] The Lord's angels take no orders from us (see Checklist chapter). They work with us and cooperate with us but their commander is God and Jesus who leads the Lord's Army.[31] We request and they are sent. Often they turn up sent but not requested to help.

Read these passages for more insight:
1 Peter 3:22
Psalm 103:20-21
Matthew 25:31
Revelation 14:10
Numbers 20:16
Daniel 3:17-18
Acts 12:11

Some angels are around to have fun with us. Some are warriors, some harvester angels, some messenger and some angels of breakthrough. Other angels are our guardians. People have seen many different ones. They are seen in human form and in angelic form.

Fallen angels (demons) who report to the accuser can be ordered away by us.[32] I am sure satanists can use them. The Lord's angels fight them and defend us against them.[33]

Warriors believe in signs and wonders, miracles, deliverance, healing and salvation. Salvation is the greatest miracle of all.[34]

They know that if they do not strive, the Lord does all the work. They have nothing to prove to Him. Their Leader loves them for who they are, not what they have achieved.[35] The original skill sets they have received came from Him. Their duty is solely to do His will, praise and worship Him and give Him thanks. This is a pretty cool task.

If warriors use the talents He has given them and multiply them for His purpose, He delights in them.[36]

Warriors together are like the crew on an ocean racing yacht in rough seas and high winds. They look out for each other at all times. They think of their colleagues and watch and listen. Like an SAS or DELTA team, they are self-sufficient, inter-dependent and spiritually, emotionally, intellectually and physically fit.

They know when they need rest to restore their energy. They also know when they can work out of the overflow.

Warriors are servant leaders, leading by example, not from control or force.[37] Humble, they put the other person first.

There is a school of thought that one has to be absolutely ascetic and puritanical to live the correct moral life to be acceptable to God. This is no more false than the person who goes to other extremes of hedonism and enjoyment. There is a very happy medium in which the two can co-exist whilst we are on the path to perfection.

Care does have to be taken in the area of having 'clean hands and a pure heart' (Psalm 24:3-4), as the enemy takes great pleasure in dragging souls back into slavery. This type of slavery is in areas of addiction such as sexual excess, drugs, gambling, alcohol etc.

One just needs to be aware of anything that takes away a person's self-control.

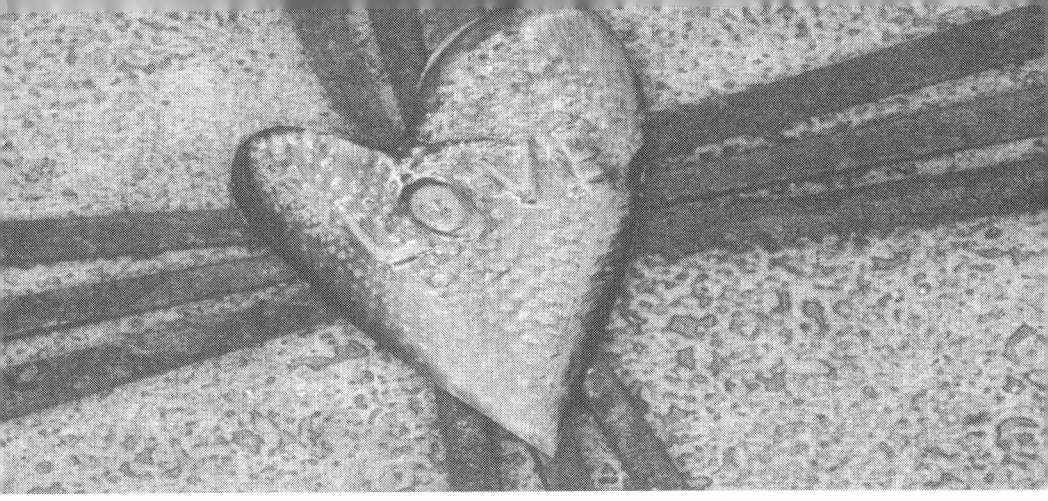

PARADISE LOST

Whoever acknowledges me before others, I will also acknowledge before my Father in heaven. But whoever disowns Me before others, I will disown before My Father in heaven. Matthew 10:32-33

LIFE UNREDEEMED

This is a brief testimony of my life before redemption.

I was adopted at the age of three months into a loving family (the Meyrick's) from a Catholic orphanage in London.

My mother Esme Kathleen Jones was a Welsh chambermaid who worked in Bournemouth. My birth father remains unknown, though my adoptive father mentioned that he had been told he was a chef!

So, I am half Welsh. My birth grandfather was a Borough engineer for Bournemouth and hailed from Newport in Wales.

My adoptive sister, Sarah arrived three years later, an 'Irish Coleen' with a fiery spirit.

I researched my birth late. Only in 2004 was I given my real birth certificate that my parents had withheld, probably out of fear, bless them.

I was brought up as a Roman Catholic and went to private schools; All Hallows Preparatory School, and Ampleforth College in Yorkshire. The

Benedictine way of teaching had an enormous effect on me with its calm, wise, eclectic and friendly approach. I grew up with a deep love for the arts, literature, history of the world and people. There was always a monk that had an interest or skill in just about any sport, pastime or pursuit.

I chose fly-fishing, shooting and individual sports: sailing, skiing, fencing, tennis and swimming.

Naturally at school I suffered some teasing and bullying once I had revealed my origins. There were however many good friends in both schools who protected me. I seemed always to get on with elder boys who kept a 'weather eye'. It would take a long time for me to learn to 'guard my heart'. My housemasters verged from the eccentric to the sublimely humble and mild.

In all, I have very happy memories of this time and although I nearly plumped for immediate monasticism I had a good mentor in Father Dominic Milroy who told me to "be off and taste the world!"

I had had a very ardent faith and belief in the Godhead. I never really related to the Holy Spirit. He was a bit of a mystery.

Mary, The mother of Jesus was made to feature strongly and was always woven into my night prayers. She has come now to represent amazing purity, grace, patience and wonder at her obedience to the Lord. A most blessed personage who carried a prophecy silently for decades about her Son. However, I have since learned I do not need to intercede via her to her Son. We forget she was anointed with the Holy Spirit in the room upstairs and was a warrior bride too.

My adopted family - hereafter referred to as 'family'- was very nautical with two admirals, and numerous senior officers.

My father retired from a distinguished Naval career as Captain 'passed over' for promotion by a disgruntled admiral. I grew up loving sailing and respecting the elements.

My paternal grandmother, 'Cuckoo', adored me and showered me with her love.

My mother, Sue, who converted to Catholicism, had also been adopted and had lost her parents just after the war. For sixty-nine wonderful years she was married to my father, Tim, the scion of the family. He was outgoing, generous, loving, charismatic, disciplined and had a strong faith rooted in the practices of the Anglican Church.

As in all upper middle class Victorian families there was the element of stiff upper lip. However, I was under no illusion that I was blessed and was very fortunate not to be languishing in foster homes.

My relationship with God was distant and not truly personal.

In 1974 I qualified as a Chartered Accountant and shortly after sailed across the Atlantic to the New World, ending up in Bermuda for three years.

As a Catholic I grew up devout, in attendance at church, serving as an acolyte and delighting in the pomp and ceremony. I had tasted the simplicity of the way of St. Benedictine, and the splendour of the high altar at Arundel with bishops and senior clergy all around. I was honoured to know two heads of the Catholic Church personally. God was working on me slowly and stealthily.

Ironically, I had not learned about the necessity of adhering to Psalm 24:3-4, having 'clean hands and a pure heart'. I lacked a deep sense of spirituality.

Sinning was relatively easy, so long as I went and confessed after. I remember someone saying to me recently "As a sinner 'unsaved' we know no better, so we do not know 'the state of grace.' As a saved saint we know when we are sinning or transgressing". There is a stark difference.

It explains why the 'pick and mix' 'M and M' sweet philosophy arises in denominational Christianity. We discard the distasteful and choose the easy route.

We 'praise' the Lord on Sundays and sleep with girlfriends or boyfriends or sniff cocaine on Monday, without an ounce of remorse or guilt. Quite often because we do not realise it is wrong. It is not entirely surprising the unbelievers, Muslims and Jews look at us with disdain and incredulity as to our integrity.

Rarely do Christians 'walk the walk' or are they capable of 'talking the talk' well either.

I am still shocked by the bigotry of people not abhorring abortion, which is murder in most cases, and yet they are sickened at a child being raped or killed by a pederast. Apparently there is equipment available today that shows a lifelike person in the womb at three days old from conception! Is this not proof of life?

I was a 'conditional' Christian and not an 'unconditional' one. I set the rules that suited me. I kept God 'in a box' and made sure He stayed there. Not that I would have ever recognised this double standard.

The devil was a fact for me. He was a part of the Bible but never really encountered by me. Well, he was so firmly planted inside of me; it is not surprising I did not see him on the outside!

Strangely, I had had a fascination with the occult at school, and once or twice I had practiced Ouija and Tarot. I feared and respected the occult when I was young. Although I was fairly unaware of it, The Lord had given me a great gift of discernment of good and evil.

I never forget the story an elderly monk told me at school that was an authorised exorcist. Sent to Africa, he had been preparing and fasting to deliver a demon-possessed young boy. Not surprisingly, the local witch doctor had failed. As a precaution, aware that the exiting spirits can 'jump ship' and enter others, the monk had placed a dead pig carcass beside the child on the ground. Within seconds of the final words of exorcism, the pig's body was a mass of seething maggots and all the skin disappeared to leave just bones! A cautionary tale I never forgot.

Do not mess with evil.

Our challenge is to define this evil. Is the Lord defining evil, or are we defining it, and how much do we water it down?

I married a wonderful woman, Ali, in 1984 after years of being a dilettante bachelor, with a weakness for women. Ali bore us three lovely blessed daughters and for most of our married life outwardly, it was a charmed marriage. She was and is an excellent mother and a worthy wife. However inside me, the predator and religious bigot remained.

The enemy only comes out when we allow him to. We have to be aware he is truly resident first. In 2004 I fell on my sword, having been unfaithful for the second time, and there was no turning back. I had let down and dishonoured my wife and my girls. There was no excuse. It needed repentance and full-scale renewal. I could not do it in my own strength.

Friends split loyalties. Some of my closest friends spurned me notwithstanding their own foibles and past failings. Some were so loyal and forgiving, bless them, they carried me along a path towards salvation. It gives me little comfort to see so many other friends going through divorce since. My parents were sympathetic and relatively non-judgemental.

I continued to carry on high-powered financial roles as Finance Director or CFO of large groups on an international scale. I had grown a large successful computer group in the 1980's that eventually succumbed to the crash in 1990.

My ego was less dented than it should have been. I still had a sense of self-worth.

An extraordinary confession to a parish priest in a graveyard was cathartic and releasing. It got me half way to recognising my plight.

On 21 November 2004, while living in a room belonging to some fabulous friends, Nigel and Jane, in a house in Clapham, London, my friend, Elise from Switzerland rang me. "I am over this weekend. Will you come with me to a church called 'Hillsong' on Sunday? I hear the music is great".

I said yes, and on Sunday morning we went to the Mermaid Theatre at Blackfriars in London where six hundred people were crammed into the auditorium.

There were many young and cheerful, friendly souls. I was captivated by the music and started to sing with gusto. Towards the end, an Australian pastor, Timmy, asked those who wanted to turn back to Christ to put their hands up. With all eyes closed and my head bowed I waited. The next thing I knew I was looking at my left hand held high in the air with a gold thread tied around the second and third finger. What was it doing up there? I could not get it down.

At once an overpowering weight started to drain from me. All my sins came before my eyes, like a DVD playing frame by frame, as my true state was revealed to me in front of the Lord. "Do you remember this" he said "and that?" Liar, bigot, the lust, the deceit. Undone I sobbed and sobbed, and hugged Elise. I felt forgiveness and love like a mass of rain flowing over me as I said sorry for everything. It was an indescribable event.

I do not think I will ever experience the like again. His love was immense like waves of warmth. It was overpowering. My knees buckled and I nearly fell.

I was given a Bible by the 'Bible man' Kris and whisked across to the nearby pub to be welcomed into the fold by friendly faces. Kathy Pavid became a good friend and eventually I took over her connect group and ran it for three years.

The Holy Spirit had chosen His moment to pounce and ambush me, and nothing that the enemy could do would stop it.

One other miracle later on in the day occurred in the family. Gemma my eldest, emerged unscathed from an upside down Fiat Panda, that had got out of control in her hands on an icy road on Goodwood Hill in Sussex. Thank you Lord.

Day one - new beginnings.

PARADISE REGAINED

For even the Son of Man did not come to be served, but to serve, and to give his life as a ransom for many. Mark 10:45

Surprise! Surprise! God did not create the Universe in a day nor is our life changed on day two except that we know we are saved and start to realise the love that our Maker has for us.

'Day Two of salvation' may be the antithesis and anit-climax, why? Well, the enemy has just lost a soul back to God. I had the misfortune not to have anyone around to take me through Bootcamp (See Chapter Six).

I muddled along from what was a high, the previous day to a pretty normal median for some time. Yes, I immersed myself in church at Hillsong, joining teams and getting some wonderful fellowship. I did start reading my Bible and studying but I still was only looking at my heart in a sporadic way. As I came to find out later, we are clinically incapable of reading or seeing into our hearts.

The heart is deceitful above all things, and it is exceedingly perverse and corrupt and severely, mortally sick! Who can know it [perceive, understand, be acquainted with his own heart and mind]? I the Lord search the mind; I try the heart, even to give to every man according to his ways, according to the fruit of his doings. Jeremiah 17:9-10 AMP

In case you think that this is just Old Testament theology, it is New Testament theology as well. Have a look at: Matthew 13:15; Mark 7:21-22; Revelation 2:23.

Searching one's heart with the Lord may reveal many hidden matters that hitherto have not surfaced. For me, these included lust, pornography, fear of man, the 'orphan spirit' and rejection. This was not a bad list to get started on. Since 2004 it has taken a good few years for these spirits to be 'exorcised', 'purged' and their doors of entry closed.

Receiving ministry, prayer, mini-deliverance of particular strongholds and wearing the 'Ephesians 6' body armour 24/7 have aided majorly. I have had Sozo sessions [a tool Bethel developed for inner healing ministry] for brief check-ups. I needed to learn to honour, respect and value others. Rather than using or exploiting people, I needed to learn to just love on them. With my past, this was difficult, as I feared rejection.

The learning process I gradually went through was that I needed to rely and depend on the love of my Father in heaven, as His was an unconditional love with no hooks and agendas. I was a Son of the King, a member of the Royal Family, a Prince and part of the corporate Bride for the Bridegroom. The latter revelation has only just recently sunk in. God's love was there for me everyday and He protected me whatever storms happened on earth. I needed to learn to trust, to love unconditionally and above all, to forgive. This is the product of Grace.

To me forgiveness was the most illogical action demanded of us. Should there not be retribution on the one who has hurt us? No! Not from us. The Lord revealed very clearly the need for forgiveness. He told me to 'separate the action from the person'. Love the person, but rebuke the action. The Lord would mete out justice and mercy as He saw fit. Not me. I was learning that whatever spirits of affliction resided in the person, these acted as the catalyst for the bad action or reaction.

As He loved all of us the same, whether we were broken, lost, unloved, abused, crazy or filled with hatred, we were required to love the same. This is a challenge, but not impossible.

We have no other choice.

It was dawning on me slowly that Grace costs the giver; the receiver does not normally even deserve this grace. The Lord then took me to the parables of the Lost Coin, Sheep and Prodigal Son as great examples.

The parable of the 'unforgiving servant' was also a real eye opener. Our God is an awesome God, and He is slow to anger. However, when He sees unrighteous behaviour, especially in believers, His response may sometimes appear merciless. He is indeed the Lion and the Lamb.

'Judge not and you will not be judged'.

He is the Judge. Fortunately for us, we now have the Advocate General, Jesus, His Son, working with us as Intercessor!

"Do not judge, or you too will be judged. For in the same way you judge others, you will be judged, and with the measure you use, it will be measured to you" Matthew 7:1-2

As to forgiveness, even in the Old Testament, the Lord made its importance very clear. In the New Testament, Seventy-seven times and more was required. The Lord's Prayer is unequivocal. He doesn't forgive us unless we forgive others. Pretty scary stuff!

Then Peter came to Jesus and asked "Lord, how many times shall I forgive my brother when he sins against me? Up to seven times?' 'Jesus answered, "I tell you, not seven times, but seventy times seven." Matthew 18:21-22

In 2008 Elise and her father invited me to Lakeland, Florida with them to experience the outpouring of the Holy Spirit and Revival led by Todd Bentley and pastor Stephen Strader of Ignited Church. Revivals are characterised by a strong presence of the Holy Spirit, signs and wonders inside and outside churches.

It was in July and the 'revival outpouring' in Florida had been running since April. The main tent on the airfield was hosting ten thousand people a night and the church downtown was hosting four hundred visitors. Todd was not there the week we visited, but we heard Bobby Conner speak, and he was amazing.

So many impartations and prophetic words were spoken over me; the week went by with a whirl. Three times I was prayed over and three times I went down to the floor, 'slain in the Spirit'. I had never before experienced such an intensity of the Presence of the Lord. The air was heavy and an indescribable fragrance permeated the church. At the tent, the number of miracles and testimonies were astounding. Scoliosis was eradicated. Tumours vanished. Broken bones and chronic back injuries were healed. Metal plates disappeared. It was all new to me and frankly quite unusual. Since then, Elise's father has been cured of Crohn's disease. Praise the Lord!

The impact of Lakeland on me was gradual. I received various impartations and prophecies that I would carry a healing and deliverance ministry, and I was 'taken in hand' by the Holy Spirit. When I prayed over people they seemed to be touched. This was all new and fascinating to me, and I began to understand I was changing. I had been baptised fully in the sea at Brighton a couple of years before. It felt like a very important sealing over the past where I died to death and rose cleansed.

When I returned from Lakeland I was baptised in the Holy Spirit outside the Dominion Theatre at Tottenham Court Road. I felt gentle rain falling on me. My baptisers were in fits of laughter. I think this was when the gifts He had prepared for me started to flow.

I then got the 'revival conference' bug. I attended a 'Healing and Impartation' Course with Randy Clarke and Bill Johnson, followed by the 'Love Bristol' Conference with Mark Stibbe and Bill Johnson. Wherever there was a power evangelist conference going on, I was there.

Honour a prophet and you will get a prophet's reward.[1]

And they took offense at him. But Jesus said to them: "Only in his hometown and in his own house is a prophet without honour." Matthew 13:57

I relished the visits of James Maloney, Joshua Mills, Jerame Nelson, Gary Oates, Bobby Conner, Heidi and Rolland Baker, John and Carol Arnott, who all came to the UK at various times. I devoured books from Bethel and elsewhere, and listened to podcasts and iBethel TV.

I met Dom Muir of NowBelieve Ministries in 2009 at 'Love Bristol'. We were both flat out on the floor at a conference and he gave me his visiting card. Soon after I went on the 'Growth in the Supernatural' Course, and started going on outreach in Soho on Thursday nights.

I received many prophetic words: 'Warrior', 'minister of mercy', 'breaker of strongholds', 'bringer in of the Presence'. 'A Father figure', someone who would go 'out of his depth' in the river and take risks.

I still had to 'clean up my act.' If I wanted these anointing, I needed to become radical. It required a commitment to celibacy and a further purging of any non-kingdom stuff.

One sermon which impacted me greatly was on the CD called "You receive the Power" by Bobby Conner, on how easily the anointing could be taken away.

The story of Saul and David rang true. Intimacy with the Lord was a prerequisite for obedience, and both were essential. Cloaked rebellion was a real risk. David repented and Saul did not. Saul lost and David was restored.

It was important to listen closely, and be in alignment at all times. It was necessary to follow instructions however daft they seemed. It was important not to diverge from His purpose and timing, and to seek confirmation if unsure.

Who may ascend the hill of the Lord? Who may stand in his holy place? He who has clean hands and a pure heart, who does not lift up his soul to an idol or swear by what is false. Psalm 24:3-4

I was slowly learning it was all about Him and had nothing to do with me.

Reader, speak this out now: 'it is not about me it is all about Him'.

I started to co-labour with the Holy Spirit. As soon as I worked in my own strength I heard laughter in Heaven. He takes care of everything, He reminded me.

The trilogy Final Quest, the Call and the Torch and the Sword by Rick Joyner took me to new levels of comprehension about the end-times prophesied in the book of Revelation. The DVDs Finger of God and Furious Love showed how the Lord used His Heavenly Court, Cherubims, Seraphims, warrior angels, harvester angels, ministering angels, Special Forces, and signs that made us wonder. The back up and arsenal was endless.

I was never alone. I just needed to learn to seek His Presence then host His Presence.

In early 2010 I started to get fast-tracked. The Lord gave me a choice of two churches to join: Chiswick Christian Centre led by Phil Whitehead and Kingsgate fellowship run by Pastor Ian McCormack, affectionately known as the Jellyfish Man. I decided that Kingsgate with its fivefold ministry philosophy and strong prophetic side was best for me and Ian really wanted my 'apostle-evangelist' persona on board.

The ship was setting sail. We bathed in the 'well' at the Moravian church. 24/7 prayer started and I ran a connect group with the amazing worship team as members.

By summer 2011, I had visited Bethel church in Redding California twice and joined their Global Legacy group, an apostolic network round the world. I had got to meet Bill and Beni Johnson, Kevin, Theresa and Chad Dedmon as well as Joaquin Evans and my good friend Danny Silk. Bill and Beni were such friendly hosts on my first visit when they happened to be there. They took me to the prayer room and Danny greeted me like a long lost brother. While he was praying with me Bill jumped us both and we all landed on the floor in a heap laughing. Bethel is like my second home.

In January 2011 I booked into the Decree Conference in San Diego. Led by Jerame and Miranda Nelson, they had invited Bobby Conner, Paul Keith Davis and Jeff Jansen along to talk. What favour I received. Jerame had held me a front seat and I had dinner with them all in the green room at the end of the evening. I learned that these wonderful people were just ordinary people and should never be idolised but loved, honoured and respected.[2]

By June 2011, I had been told I had received the mantle of Nehemiah, Joseph and strangely Esther. I sought out to understand what they meant with the help of the Lord. The Nehemiah mantle is that of building and restoring: the redemptive gift of ruling. Extraordinary, as that has been my secular role as a trouble-shooter to ailing groups for twenty years, rebuilding them from ground upwards. The second, the mantle of Joseph, I am getting to grips with, but it is linked to Government and authority. The mantle of Esther is all about intercession and being a vessel for worship. The latter I adore as I dance and fly banners. I spend a lot of time as a prayer warrior as well.

Do I qualify to be a warrior? I feel so. The mantle of humility however is the most important to retain over our armour at all times. As Rick Joyner learned to his cost, when he disobeyed the Lord to show off his shiny armour by lifting his mantle of humility.

The Lord gave me dance as a worship form. Through this, He has told me I can bring in the Presence.

I got ticked off by the Lord at a Revival Alliance meeting. I had stopped dancing and had become distracted. A lady behind me gave me a message from the Lord to the effect that I needed to continue dancing to usher in the Presence. I went up to the front and started to dance again in the Spirit. The Presence arrived the Glory of the Lord fell and me too to the ground! I am sure I was only one of the ushers!

So how do you start along this road? It is a good idea to be fired up by the Great Commission Jesus gave to us:

As you go, proclaim this message: 'The kingdom of heaven has come near.' Heal the sick, raise the dead, cleanse those who have leprosy, drive out demons. Freely you have received; freely give. Matthew 10:7-8

So why enter God's army. Why not opt for a simple life?

WHY ENTER GOD'S ARMY?

> 'We have just enough religion to make us hate not enough to make us love one another.' Swift

Firstly, God has His own Heavenly Army, the Heavenly Host of angels.[1] The end time army of God on earth is comprised of disciples of Christ. The term 'Christian' evolved from the word 'disciple', an active follower and student of Christ. Christ was a Jew and there is no mention of Christian in the Bible. A Christian is 'an anointed one.' However, I believe the term now covers a multitude of types of Christian. The term 'Christian' is undoubtedly supposed to represent a true disciple.

I have since learned that with sixty three thousand denominations and churches in Chritianity, and growing, the name is fairly misleading. Jesus came to bring in His Father's Kingdom not Christianity. I prefer to say I am an ambassador for the Kingdom of Jesus or Yeshua.

So, what characterises a disciple? Whole-hearted devotion and obedience to the Lord Jesus. What frameworks does a disciple/warrior live by?[2] Self-discipline, Kingdom values and behaviours, rules, techniques, knowledge, learning and use of intelligence data, defending ones country, family values, ideals, pride in serving the people, fitness. There are many parallels with the British Army code.

In earthly armies it is possible to be a part time soldier. Sometimes civilians are called up to serve as soldiers in a war, or they may be part of a Territorial Army or Reservists. In Jesus's army there are only full time soldiers. Ephesians 6 armour is worn full time. Soldiers in Jesus's army can be operating in all arenas, lay or church. Soldiers in God's army know they are saved and have eternity with their Godhead to look forward to.[3] I am avoiding the pitfall of 'born again-ness' as I believe the Lord only knows those who are saved. You will know if you are 'born again' as it is an experiential event with the Holy Spirit. It might even be private when you give your heart to Jesus.

Some will say soldiers are all end time warriors. I disagree. The warrior is brave, experienced, fearless, freed, an unconstrained soldier.[4] Warriors are on the front line of battle and serve in the Special Forces. They walk in the gifts and mantles they have been given.

There is a big difference between carrying the mantle or office of prophet and being given prophetic gifts by the Lord. The former is a full-time role. The gift of prophecy however is given to many, but sometimes it is not fully utilised, or it can be misused.

Are you prepared to lay your life down for King and Faith? Do we have an enemy to fight?

Ephesians 6:12 has a stark message to all who want to absorb it and enter God's army and be a warrior: *For our struggle is not against flesh and blood, but against the rulers, against the authorities, against the powers of this dark world and against the spiritual forces of evil in the heavenly realms.*

Remember the story of Lucifer [the true name of the devil is 'heylel' according to Isaiah 14:12 in the Hebrew, and uninfluenced by the Illuminati trying to glorify him].

How have you fallen from heaven, O [a light-bringer and daystar, son of the morning! How you have been cut down to the ground, you who weakened and laid low the nations [O blasphemous, satanic king of Babylon!] And you said in your heart, I will ascend to heaven; I will exalt my throne above the stars of God; I will sit upon the mount of assembly in the uttermost north. I will ascend above the heights of the clouds; I will make myself like the Most High. Isaiah 14:12-14 AMP

"Son of man, take up a lament concerning the king of Tyre and say to him: 'this is what the Sovereign LORD says: 'You were the seal of perfection, full of wisdom and perfect in beauty. You were in Eden, the garden of God; every precious stone adorned you: carnelian, chrysolite and emerald, topaz, onyx and jasper, lapis lazuli, turquoise and beryl. Your settings and mountings were made of gold; on the day you were created they were prepared. You were anointed as a guardian cherub, for so I ordained you. You were on the holy mount of God; you walked among the fiery stones. You were blameless in your ways from the day you were created till wickedness was found in you. Through your widespread trade you were filled with violence, and you sinned. So I drove you in disgrace from the mount of God, and I expelled you, guardian cherub, from among the fiery stones. Your heart became proud on account of your beauty, and you corrupted your wisdom because of your splendour. So I threw you to the earth; I made a spectacle of you before kings. By your many sins and dishonest trade you have desecrated your sanctuaries. So I made a fire come out from you, and it consumed you, and I reduced you to ashes on the ground in the sight of all who were watching." Ezekiel 28:12-18

Heylel (the devil) was an Archangel alongside Michael, Gabriel and others. They were right hand beings in the presence of God. He was extremely beautiful and the closest to God. Due to pride, arrogance and vanity, he chose to challenge the Almighty's authority and Jesus in particular.[5] A rebellion broke out in Heaven. heylel (the illuminate name meaning 'light and morning star') and one third of the heavenly host at that time were cast out of Heaven to the cosmos including earth, never to return. Sin entered the world.[6]

heylel and the fallen angels arrived on earth in the pre-Adamic age, long before Eden and causing the Ice Age. Scripture enlighten us about the fall into the cosmos, in Isaiah 14:22.

heylel managed to fool Eve and Adam, convincing them they needed to eat of the fruit of the knowledge of good and evil in order to be true sons of God. This was the lie. They were already fully in His likeness. heylel regained dominion over earth given to Adam.

About eight hundred years later, this caused God to restart the world again with the flood. In the days of Noah and his family, who were the only set-apart holy descendants God left on earth to start life again, the devil managed, with man's agreement, to wed demons to man causing further carnage.[7]

Though dominion was lost, it has now been recovered by Jesus.[8] But the enemy continues to plague man with ungodly behaviours.[9]

The war in the heavenlies has long been completed though battles and skirmishes continue.[10] That is why heylel can only be beaten in the spirit real by using the power of the Almighty to bring Heaven to Earth along with His heavenly host of angels.[11] We cannot take him and his hordes on in earthly form. Jesus, by his sacrifice, bought back earth for us.[12] Sadly most still believe the world belongs to satan.

We need spiritual armament. Hence we fight the battle in the spiritual realm that sits between the third Heaven and us. That is why the armour of Elohim (Light=God) is to be worn at all times. At the start of the following Bible passage it shows us what we are up against.

THE ARMOUR OF GOD

Finally, be strong in the Lord and in his mighty power. Put on the full armour of God, so that you can take your stand against the devil's schemes. For our struggle is not against flesh and blood, but against the rulers, against the authorities, against the powers of this dark world and against the spiritual forces of evil in the heavenly realms. Therefore put on the full armour of God, so that when the day of evil comes, you may be able to stand your ground, and after you have done everything, to stand. Stand firm then, with the belt of truth buckled around your waist, with the breastplate of righteousness in place, and with your feet fitted with the readiness that comes from the gospel of peace. In addition to all this, take up the shield of faith, with which you can extinguish all the flaming arrows of the evil one. Take the helmet of salvation and the sword of the Spirit, which is the word of God. And pray in the Spirit on all occasions with all kinds of prayers and requests. With this in mind, be alert and always keep on praying for all the Lord's people. Ephesians 6:10-18

DO YOU REALLY WANT TO JOIN?

Danny Silk from Bethel Church, Redding, California runs a series for people thinking of getting married. It is called 'Defining the Relationship.' He starts with the intention of deterring and upsetting course participants who are contemplating marriage. Obstacles and challenges appear and the faint hearted fall early. He plans to put thirty to forty percent of couples off getting married. He talks of the 'La La La' factor that we all catch when we fall in love. The 'rose tinted glasses' are removed rapidly. Are people common in their purpose and aims? Where will the friction points be? Do they respect and honour each other?

A similar commitment is required when joining the Lord of Lords' Army. There can be no desertion once you join.

Similar to earthly forces, generals cannot do much with prisoners of war or captives held for ransom. It is pretty difficult to get to troops that have been taken captive. They are not front line material, let alone of much use until freed from their captors.

Earthly impediments or strongholds where you are still held captive by the enemy make you 'easy picking' and 'walking wounded.'

Anger, fear, frustration, unresolved issues, unforgiveness, jealousy, hatred, inability to receive love or give it, pride, vanity, lust, greed are the weaponry of satan and have no place in the Kingdom army.

However, if you have compassion, forgiveness, a love for people, grace, generosity, humour, a touch of the clown, lack of self-conciousness and no fear of man, this is promising.

Age is irrelevant in the Kingdom.[13] Our past life is irrelevant[14] and often the murkier it has been, the more you 'bring to the party'! Ethnicity, language, culture, upbringing are all levellers and equally, are not an impediment.[15]

If you are looking for a comfortable ride, then do not join! If you are looking for full-time excitement and immediate gratification, be warned. Joining the King's army has a Kingdom health warning. Unlike victorious soldiers and brave ones in our earthly forces, glory hunting is taboo and definitely 'out'. All the glory goes to the King of Kings. We will be lifted up, by having the sole motive in our hearts to uplift the Lord in everything.[16]

The Kingdom army is a place of paradox. All the topsy-turvy words of Jesus come true.

The last will indeed be first. The humble will be exalted and the exalted will be humbled. The meek inherit the most and forgiveness is a pre-requisite. 'Turning the other cheek' is the first response to attack and we lose everything to gain the Eternal.

Our bank account and reward is in Heaven and not here on earth.

We learn to rest in storms and be active in peaceful times.[17] Patience is not only a virtue, it's 'de rigeur'.

Our weaponry of loving, forgiving and praising is strange and alien, but once one is acclimatised to it, it is simple to use.

Instructions sometimes come down in riddles from the Throne.[18] Orders may be given at three in the morning. Commands may not be logical but you challenge them at risk. God may use code to be deciphered. (It is the glory of God to conceal a matter).[19]

I love the poem 'IF' by Rudyard Kipling. If you model the qualities captured in this poem, you are a likely candidate for enrolment.

> If you can keep your head when all about you are losing theirs
> And blaming it on you,
> If you can trust yourself when all men doubt you,
> But make allowance for their doubting too;
>
> If you can wait and not be tired by waiting,

WHY ENTER THE LORD'S ARMY

Or being lied about, don't deal in lies,
Or being hated, don't give way to hating,
And yet don't look too good, nor talk too wise:

If you can dream - and not make dreams your master;
If you can think - and not make thoughts your aim;
If you can meet with Triumph and Disaster
And treat those two impostors just the same;

If you can bear to hear the truth you've spoken
Twisted by knaves to make a trap for fools,
Or watch the things you gave your life to, broken,
And stoop and build 'em up with worn-out tools:

If you can make one heap of all your winnings
And risk it on one turn of pitch-and-toss, and lose,
And start again at your beginnings
And never breathe a word about your loss;

If you can force your heart and nerve and sinew
To serve your turn long after they are gone,
And so hold on when there is nothing in you
Except the Will, which says to them: 'Hold on!'

If you can talk with crowds and keep your virtue,
Or walk with Kings - nor lose the common touch,
If neither foes nor loving friends can hurt you,
If all men count with you, but none too much;

If you can fill the unforgiving minute
With sixty seconds' worth of distance run,
Yours is the Earth and everything that's in it,

And - which is more - you'll be a Man, my son!

You will be hated by some and marginalized by others. You will be misunderstood by some, misconstrued by many and mystifying to the rest.

WHAT ARE THE SPIRITS THAT OPPOSE THE ARMY OF GOD?
The spirits of hell:
Lucifer- Pride
Mammon- Greed
Asmodeus - Lust
Satan- Wrath
Beelzebub (also called Baal) - Gluttony
Leviathan - Envy
Belphegor- Vanity and Sloth

These spirits that manifested in Cain, Delilah, Jezebel, David and the King of Tyre can suddenly rise up against you. They can 'sit on top of' people you know, love and trust and attempt to take you out or discredit you. Friends you have had for years may well shun you.

Are you still enthusiastic?

WHAT ARE THE BENEFITS?
You make some fabulous friends for life. You help to hasten the destruction of the enemy and restore Heaven's dominion over earth with the coming of Christ in the millennium reign. We are now in the time of the Laodocian church, written of in the book of Revelation.

You have the pleasure of people you love and respect being saved and restored into a rightful relationship with their loving Creator.

You co-labour with the Lord, a mighty honour and privilege. You use His power responsibly and obediently and get to experience a lot of joy in the process!

You receive favour beyond what you can comprehend, and protection for all your loved ones.

You sense, savour and feel at first hand His vast overflowing love and unconditional adoration. This has no parallel or comparison. You have access to Him every day and are able to soak in His Presence.

No drug rush, orgasm or adrenaline shot can even measure minutely against the feeling of the overwhelming power of His love for those who are close to Him!

Your reward in Heaven will be great. As we have only a little time on earth compared to eternity, this seems like a very attractive proposition. If this has not whetted your appetite for more, stop reading now.

BASIC QUALIFICATIONS

Very truly I tell you, no servant is greater than his master, nor is a messenger greater than the one who sent him. John 13:16

These qualifications might seem obvious but they are not. As I have said before, age, culture, socio-economic group, ethnicity, denomination, colour, health, disabilities play no part. He chooses healthy and ill people, people who cannot read or write, dyslexic, disphraxic, men and women. They are not all alpha types.[1] Many have not gone to bible school or divinity colleges or indeed are steeped in bible verses.

One common denominator appears to be having a passion for seeking the Presence and wanting a close personal relationship with their Maker.

Another qualification is the person has finally realised they cannot work through their own strength but only in obedience and under instruction with the weaponry from the Lord.[2]

I come across so many people trying to do ministry in their own strength, physically pushing pressing and generally working completely outside the remit of the Holy Spirit. This is akin to using witchcraft and very dangerous.[3]

I remember one location where there was a person praying words over me, and my Spirit and reacted as they were utterly non-kingdom and made up of an amalgam of personal agendas and home-spun truths.

James Goll in The Lost Art of Intercession refers to the Word he received from God: God said "I'm going to teach you to release the highest weapon of spiritual warfare. I'm going to teach you to release the brilliance of My great presence."

What is the highest weapon of spiritual warfare? Why it is God himself! People who have learned this, have the basic qualification.

There are some caveats about launching without checking if you match the criteria. It can appear quite gung-ho and trendy to be doing this. Friends are doing it and there is peer pressure to follow. Going to outreaches in 'badlands' is a good thing.

Do you have the stomach for failure? Are you really fearless or just talking it? Do you fold under criticism? Do you fly off the handle easily?

Are you very sensitive or self-conscious? Are you ready for attack? Are you able to talk the Gospel story in simple short sentences? Are you child-like in nature?

Do you love testimonies and like to tell them? Do you pray regularly everyday? Do you aspire to a holiness of heart? Do you believe you are empowered to use the Keys we have been given? Do you have an unwavering faith?

Are you an extravagant giver? Are you a servant leader? Are you prepared to be humbled?

I know people rather 'bang on' about being a 'born again' Christian. It sounds just like another label and seems no different from a Roman Catholic differing themselves from being Christian.[4]

I prefer to listen to what the Lord said to me the other day. 'KISS' -'Keep it Simple Son!'. His message and lifestyle should be simple and we should follow His example.

Act out the first two commandments given to Moses.

'Teacher, which is the greatest commandment in the Law?" Jesus replied: 'Love the Lord your God with all your heart and with all your soul and with your entire mind. This is the first and greatest commandment. And the second is like it too: 'Love your neighbour as yourself. All the Law and the

BASIC QUALIFICATIONS

Prophets hang on these two commandments." Matthew 22:37-40

Christ, God 'made man',5 went through full immersion baptism which clearly pleased His Father.6 It was at this point that He was publicly affirmed and proclaimed by His Father, God, as being His son. The Holy Spirit fell upon Him and he received the fullness of Holy Spirit.[6]

The water baptism drowned him symbolically of all earthly evil.[7] He died to death in the earthly terms.[8] He was 'Born again'. The baptism of the Holy Spirit gave Him the arsenal to walk in the full power of God again on earth.[9] The Power resided inside him. He was affirmed as God's Son, as we are.[10]

He had come down from a glorified state where he existed in the Trinity before time began to become man and this is why he did this.

If He had come as God, we would never be able to do what He did. It is because He became man completely, we are enabled to do what He did.[11]

That is why he said to his followers in Matthew 16:19 *"I will give you the keys of the kingdom of heaven; whatever you bind on earth will be bound in heaven, and whatever you loose on earth will be loosed in heaven"*

"I tell you the truth; anyone who has faith in me will do what I have been doing. He will do even greater things than these, because I am going to the Father." John 14:12

NOTICE, THIS IS A MANDATE. It follows as the other Davidian Key given in prophecy by Isaiah:

I will place on his shoulder the key to the house of David; what he opens no one can shut, and what he shuts no one can open. Isaiah 22:22 and Revelation 3:7

We have these keys at our fingertips. This will be expalined in the toolkit chapter later.

It may also help you to enrol on a supernatural ministry course.

NowBelieve runs a course in London called Growth in the Supernatural. This is a series of twelve evening meetings, with a detailed handbook to study.

NowBelieve goes out to Soho most Thursday nights to minister to the lost.

In the States, Bethel Church in Redding California have a School of

Supernatural Ministry run by Bill Johnson, Kris Vallotton and Danny Silk. There are many others including Randy Clark's, are all excellent training grounds. Paul Keith Davis runs a monthly School of the Spirit that is available online, as does Doctor O (Bishop Adonijah Ogbonnaya) and many other notable men of God.

There are UK schools too. North Kent Community Church, run by Peter Carter, uses the Bethel Church model. HOTS 'Healing on the streets' in the UK is breaking out everywhere and is a great practicing ground.

Enough has been said on qualifications. The Lord will reveal to you His purpose for you. Just ask Him.[12]

THE OPPOSITION

The devil's boots don't creak. Scottish Proverb

This chapter took some time to write as I had real resistance to its content being revealed. It is important that you pray protection and cover over yourself as you read and when you have finished it or dipped in, you cleanse yourself of any negative or fear 'cling-ons'.

What you focus on in life focuses on you.[1] We must never put the enemy or his actions on a pedestal or dwell too long on him. He is defeated and lost and through the Blood of the Lamb we beat him at every corner.[2] However, as an adversary, he should be taken seriously, recognising the power he can have over lost or misguided souls.[3]

The enemy only has power where man has agreed to share it with him. He only has dominion where we have enabled him to have dominion in all the spheres of the Kingdom.

In Luke 4 the enemy offered Jesus not just one kingdom but kingdoms; that intimates there are many.

I have covered a little bit on the enemy previously, and what his plans are and how he works. Let us look at this in more detail.

What does Jesus say about the devil and what we should be doing?[4]

I have given you authority to trample on snakes and scorpions and to overcome all the power of the enemy; nothing will harm you. Luke 10:19

And these signs will accompany those who believe: In my name they will drive out demons; they will speak in new tongues; Mark 16:17

..that at the name of Jesus every knee should bow, in heaven and on earth and under the earth, Philippians 2:10

...and do not give the devil a foothold. Ephesians 4:27

Submit yourselves, then, to God. Resist the devil, and he will flee from you. James 4:7

Be self-controlled and alert. Your enemy the devil prowls around like a roaring lion looking for someone to devour. Resist him, standing firm in the faith, because you know that your brothers throughout the world are undergoing the same kind of sufferings. 1 Peter 5 8-9

It is clear we have power over the devil and he, like everyone, should be forced to bow to the Lord. The question is do we believe it? What are the underlying messages in these verses?

The enemy has been defeated in the spiritual world.[5] We can only have him flee from us, if we work in faith.[6] We are given authority to take him on when we speak in Jesus's name. This is the key. Never claim in our name.[7]

So how does the 'enemy' gain toeholds, footholds and strongholds in humans? The answer is pretty easily: By us being in agreement with him.

God is Good,

God is Love,

God is All-Powerful.

God is the Great 'I Am'.

He was, is and always shall be.

He is outside time.

Where there is negativity, wrong, illness, anger, frustration, fear, impatience: in fact all things negative, there you will find the presence of evil.

We are vessels to be filled by God and infused with the Holy Spirit. Where we allow other concoctions to enter into our bloodstream, oxygen and body whether in thought, word or deed that are non-Godly there the enemy resides.

Nature abhors a vacuum.

The enemy comes to kill, steal and destroy.[8] He resides in the spiritual realm between Heaven and us. Although unable to read our mind,[9] unfortunately for us, he can read, see and hear everything else. He can enter artifacts, pictures, emblems, clothing, rooms, and of course bodies. The enemy can cling on outside, or he is comfortably inside us. He can work in the ether, through transmission of touch, the web, TV, films, in fact, all matters. He is most effective coming out of people's mouths.

You use your mouth for evil and harness your tongue to deceit. Psalm 50:19

The tongue has the power of life and death, and those who love it will eat its fruit. Proverbs 18:21

There is so much power in the tongue and when the enemy takes control of it, havoc can be wrought. 'Put-downs' are curses. Telling a child they will never be a success is a demonic curse. Calling someone stupid is a curse. Repent of it now! God loves His children and is not the slightest bit worried about what they end up doing if they do 'good' for His purpose and are happy and loving.

Now can you start to see if the enemy has any residual influence on your life, look to yourself first, and then you can look elsewhere. As Christ said:

How can you say to your brother, 'Brother, let me take the speck out of your eye,' when you yourself fail to see the plank in your own eye? You hypocrite, first take the plank out of your eye, and then you will see clearly to remove the speck from your brother's eye. Luke 6:47

So where does he manifest easily? In people who are weak-willed or are lacking grace.[10] People with addictions. If they are captive to that spirit, the spirit is one of his minions. Gluttony, envy, idolatry, lust, anger, hatred, sloth. Do keep in mind that He sees the sin, but loves the sinner.

In the Book of Proverbs, the Lord mentions six things He hates and one He detests:

A proud look.

A lying tongue.

Hands that shed innocent blood.

A heart that devises wicked plots.

Feet that are swift to run into mischief.

A deceitful witness that utters lies.

A man who sows discord among brethren

Galatians 5:19-21 includes more of the traditional seven sins, although the list is substantially longer: adultery, fornication, uncleanness, lasciviousness, idolatry, sorcery, hatred, variance, emulations, wrath, strife, seditions, heresies, envyings, murders, drunkenness, revellings, and such like.

So now we know where he resides. In actions, thoughts and deeds. Does he manifest physically? Yes, from time to time. Is it scary? Yes. Can he take over personalities and people completely? Yes. Is Schizophrenia sometimes demonic? Yes. Has he been known to command the elements? Yes.

In Mark 4:35-41 is the story of the storm at sea whipped up by the enemy, where Jesus slept and was woken to calm the storm. satan did not want Jesus and the disciples getting to the land of Gaderenes as it was an area and country where satan had complete dominion over. The naked madman there called himself 'Legion'. Two thousand demons came out of him and on the demons request, were allowed to go into pigs. The pigs all rushed over the side of the bank and drowned in the lake.

The Case of the drop of black ink.

This is an account of something that happened in a Soho-ministry outreach one evening. We were preparing ourselves through prayer, and the anointing was very strong. A couple, middle-aged and dressed in dark clothing, walked by. The man stretched out his arm and touched one of the girls in our team just below the left shoulder. They moved off and the man started to shake and jiggle. The Lord nudged me. I knew immediately what had happened. He had received the anointing!

The girl felt like an ice pick had touched her arm and it was very cold and unpleasant. The couple had moved across to the entrance of a big shop. They turned back and were waving at me. I followed them into the shop. When they turned to face me I told them to never come back here and do not ever touch my friends again. The man told me they wanted some of the anointing that my friend carried.

They proceeded to tell me they believed in God but worked for the other side - they were satanists. Then the power of God came on me very strongly and I rebuked them in the name of the Lord Jesus Christ, telling them again they must never come back here and you must leave this area and us in peace." They shuffled and moved backwards. As I turned to walk away she told me I was very arrogant but I replied that I was speaking in the name of the Lord Jesus Christ.

I turned and walked towards the door, there was a big security guard looking at me. The Lord told me he was a Christian. As I went by I pointed out the two people who were satanists and asked him to ensure that they left the store quickly and do not come in our direction. Such was the authority, the Lord had given me at that moment, and he obeyed like a soldier!

I returned to the team who were praying. I asked for some words of knowledge and young Micah saw a small drop of black ink that had gone into the girl's bloodstream. I started to pray and excise the poison cleansing with the Blood of the Lamb. Within a minute, her arm was shaking, and she felt whatever it was leaving through her fingertips. God is swift to act!

A few minutes later after we thanked and praised the Lord, she told me she had been given an arm of steel. What a gift?!

I got a 'word' about wasp sting and pondered on it. I remembered ten years earlier, a family member of mine had been stung in the summer by a wasp. One month later she was stung again and had an anaphylactic fit. The physician advised a fairly new technique of a two year program of microscopic injections of wasp serum which builds up resistance. Now, if she is stung it's like a gnat bite!

So here is the wondrous lesson. Despite the enemy trying to perpetrate evil, the Lord cannot only reverse but use evil to his purpose, and bring a ten-fold payback.[11]

By the way, well aware I was going to be under attack, my Harley Street Bob bike was stolen from the outside of the O2 Arena a few days later. That night I returned in a taxi and by the time I had got home, the cabbie had given his life to the Lord. So a bike was lost and a soul was saved. The story ends even better as I had full value insurance cover and the Lord led me to a new Street Warrior bike £2000 cheaper, one year older, and better. 'Amazing Grace' and 'payback' by the Father.[12]

A word on Spiritual warfare: The enemy has been defeated. Laughter and light is the best way to keep away darkness. See John 8:12.

By now you will have an idea if you want to join God's army and before signing up, you will need to go through a bit of Bootcamp.

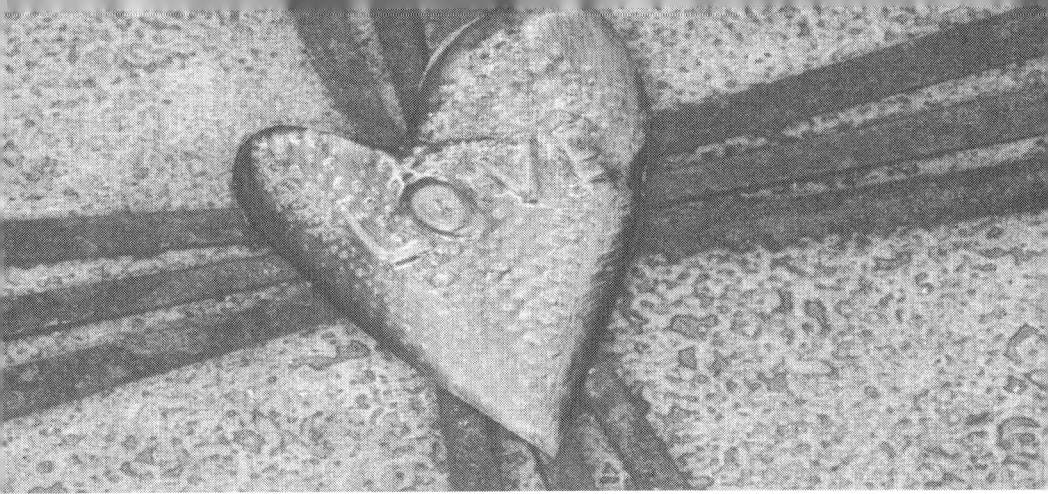

BOOTCAMP

Make me chaste and continent but not just yet! St Augustine

Boot camp refers colloquially to military recruit training. What is boot-camp supposed to teach us?

I love the film Police Academy as it parodies individuals who have volunteered to join boot-camp from all walks of life. They appear complete misfits and indeed are to start with. Slowly they get honed into a fairly effective force despite their shortcomings. Their leader is Commandant Lasard. His arch-enemy, Commandant Mauser, is elitist, jealous, over-competitive, cheating, conniving and a control freak. These are some good parallels to draw from.

Are we up for the tasks, profession or jobs we may face upon joining? Yes or No? Boot Camp teaches us to know ourselves better; It teaches us to 'Address the roots to see the fruits.'

We quickly learn we cannot do much on our own. We learn that tried and tested techniques are sensible to apply before branching out into the unknown.

We learn how to get along with others and become interdependent on each other. We learn to work in teams. We learn to follow leaders and obey commands.

We learn about the force we are joining. What is its purpose and role? We learn about the weaponry. We learn about warfare. We learn about survival and looking after ourselves. We learn strategy. We learn stealth.

We learn how to get fit and stay fit. We learn how to travel far and over tough terrain. We learn how to endure hardship. We learn about suffering pain and withstanding it. We learn about how to heal and repair people.

We learn about fairness and mercy.[1] We learn to protect the vulnerable. We learn to fight.[2] We learn to be fearless.[3] We learn to be humbled before we are exalted.[4] We learn to accept criticism and learn from mistakes rapidly.[5] We learn to improvise and innovate. We learn to protect ourselves and guard our hearts.[6]

We learn patience, and how to deal with boredom.[7] We learn how to act in the 'zone.' We learn how to forgive unconditionally.[8]

The term 'boot-camp' came to me one day when a friend of mine struggling with life's vicissitudes reached out for help. Everything seemed to be going wrong at once. Why? Was God angry with her, as she felt? Was the enemy harassing her? Was she in correction from the Lord? Nothing was clear.

She loved Him, she felt, and was pursuing a path of obedience as far as she could see. I became a sort of co-labourer with the Holy Spirit, as a boot-camp mentor, she said. We were 'Taking the lie out of the alibi' as they say in the USA.

Intelligent, gifted and beautiful as well as ambitious and driven, she was struggling with self-doubt that the enemy had sown in to her.

Let me make something very clear here which will be repeated many times. The enemy does not spend time on 'backsliders', pagans, spiritualists, atheists and unbelievers. He has them already in his grasp.

He spends time knocking the breath out of good believers who may be struggling and has great pleasure in destroying their dreams, aspirations, wealth, health and future.

Why would he waste his time elsewhere? These are his enemy. These are the army of his arch-enemy, God Almighty. If the 'enemy' incapacitates people, their effectiveness on earth weakens, and their power fighting in the supernatural world is majorly debilitated.

Such people may have some religious strength in church but they will be almost useless operating in the Holy Spirit's power.

To be operating in His power, we must be a clean vessel - pure and unadulterated. We can only be 'kept clean' by His grace. His grace makes the sometimes harsh reality of the Truth – whether good or bad, much more bearable.

As we have seen before, what we focus on, focuses on us. If we have iconic attachments to items, people, things that are not of God, the enemy gets access. If one travels to foreign climes and returns with pagan ornaments, jewellery, paintings or receive them as gifts, be wary.

Having a dragon on your shirt or a pagan god figurine in your room will create a wrong atmosphere for the Holy Spirit to operate in. Curses can and do hang on such items.

Part of the life laundry the Lord carried out with her was going through her apartment. Every item of jewellery was laid down and she sought the Lord's blessing or disapproval over them. Her bedroom had felt permeated by chill and unease. She had been suffering illnesses, some totally illogical. She slept listlessly.

Within a few days her room and apartment had changed in presence completely. She slept better, regained her health and became far more positive. There were other areas that were health checked including any evidence of frustration, shame, anger, and ambition not in line with the Lord's. Unforgiveness, a common area of access by the enemy was checked. What the Lord needed to do was completed, and her whole demeanour changed. She was happier, more confident as a vessel for the Lord to pour through. She was a warrior being prepared for battle, much better equipped. Love, generosity, compassion, always there in her nature, was able to operate effectively in the new environment.

There is a lovely continuation to this story where the Lord gave her a picture of an Ostrich egg. It was a sign of a new birth for her into a new large and exciting purpose and role He had for her. The gestation period of an Ostrich is forty-two days. She was nearly there!

If one joins the Armed Services, whether Army, Navy or Air Force, one goes through a residential course, which is principally to acclimatise one to military life. If one has not lived together with a lot of people before, this can be quite a challenge.

Similarly to sailing as crew on an ocean racer, one's kit and space is limited. Our bad habits, which we may have performed privately, now come under scrutiny in public. Whether one likes it or not, one has no choice but to get along with each other. In a boat, tacticians or skippers or lead hands scream as the crew scrambles to synchronise with what is going on.

At normal military boot-camp it is worse! Sergeants and instructors drive you on when there is nothing else left in you, testing your boundaries and horizons.

In God's army and boot-camp, it is gentler. There should be tons of love and patience and correction, but no condemnation. Boot-camp can go on for weeks or months.

It is actually in our own control and not the Lord's. We can take a breather whenever we want or 'opt out'. The Lord gives us free will. If we slide back, He waits patiently for us to come back to the Altar.

Rather like the patient Bridegroom looking back down the aisle longingly for the doors to open and His beloved to burst through, He is always there. He may sigh occasionally lovingly and knowingly. I always picture 'the Runaway Bride' film scene with Julia Roberts and Richard Gere patiently pursuing. Sadly the Lord, our Bridegroom, is used to seeing us getting 'cold feet.'[9] The Church today in the West is still a reluctant Bride!

When we complete boot-camp, the Lord's assessors will have worked out and conferred with the Lord as to what path we should perhaps take. He will already have been filling our hearts with thoughts for the future and the confirmation we are given by them will often cement the route or vocation.[10]

It may be regular army, Front Line or Special Forces. There is no shame or pecking order here. In the regular army, officers, following a campaign or battle, often select marksmen for promotion to Special Forces. The potential for some to be leaders and generals will have been spotted too, but not necessarily spoken out. Boot-camp teaches reliance on others and trust. Often some of the tests require the whole team to succeed and finish.[11] This ensures we look after the weakest of our mates or those injured.[12] The fallen are always brought back. The hand is always outstretched, but they need to grab it.

Many times in the Vietnam War, a terminally injured man elected to remain behind to create a firestorm with his last rounds to die in glory holding off and distracting the foe. The statement by Jesus for us to be prepared to lay down our lives for our brothers is very powerful.

Greater love has no one than this that he lay down one's life for one's friends. John 15:13

This is how we know what love is: Jesus Christ laid down his life for us. And we ought to lay down our lives for our brothers 1 John 3:16

Some boot-camps start without plans and one either 'dives in' or 'opts out'. People were launched into completely uncharted territory at the Indonesian Revival in 1965. In his book "Like a Mighty Wind" Mel Tari tells of getting 'cannonballed' into supernatural activity in Indonesia without any preamble.

> This was an incredible revival in a country racked with paganism, unbelief and communism. Ironically due to non-Kingdom spiritual practices, many pagans were familiar with the spirit world. Unfortunately it was just the 'wrong camp'. Their evil power was strong, as the Church had never come against them with the true firepower of the Lord of Lords.

These simple people had a baptism of fire akin to Pentecost where they were catapulted into signs and wonders on such a massive scale it was too much for some. There were no instructors, no rulebooks, and no precedents.[13] They just attempted to follow the Lord's instructions to the letter as He spoke to them.

He gave them verses of encouragement from the Bible and they always believed He would come through for them every time. He did.[14]

Poisons did not affect them.[15] They walked on water. They walked through torrential rain not getting wet.

They saw multiplication of food. There were resurrections of people. One came back to life after being dead two days! They professed their faith resolutely and praised Him. The pagans, shamans and unbelievers were converted in droves by the evidence of the Christian warriors' God and His raw power.

Some boot-camp!

Most of us have a chance to go gently with good mentoring and gradually. Some of us have been accelerated through a washing machine/spin dryer process. I am not sure which method is better.

Certainly at whatever type of 'Bootcamp' you start with, be prepared to be 'undone.'

Some could be called 'Volunteers'. They have been inspired by perhaps seeing a power evangelist in action at a conference and have suddenly felt the Presence.

They may have been going to a Pentecostal, Catholic or Anglican Church, which has prayer ministry at the end of the service. They feel called to go up for prayer and 'surprise surprise,' the Lord touches them strongly.

Maybe, they have responded to an altar call like myself, and are overcome by God's love. Their appetite is whetted. There really is a God or "what was that, that just happened?" Now the bug has been caught, it is important to start exploring. The exploration can take many forms.

Denominational churches have an approach, which differs strongly from non-denominational. There is no judgement here, as it depends on you as an individual and how comfortable you are with this new insight and environment. Some churches will suit you much better with a gentle induction into the ways of the Holy Spirit.

Holy Trinity Brompton in London has the Alpha Course that ends up with a Holy Spirit weekend. This course as an introduction to Christianity is excellent and operates worldwide.

For those more radical who want acceleration, they should apply to go to Healing and Impartation conferences. There are Schools of Supernatural Ministry that run normally for a year or two. Some can be part time, some full time.

All these environments teach one to walk and operate in His Presence.

Going on Holy Spirit Treasure Hunts and Street pastoring allows one to practice.

Boot-camp is where one makes mistakes and plenty of them. It does not matter and the more you make, the better, as you will learn from them quickly. Wisdom and understanding comes from learning from our mistakes and not repeating them.[16]

The following are two quotes by Winston Churchill:

'All men make mistakes but only wise men learn from them.'

'Success is the ability to go from one failure to another with no loss of enthusiasm.'

I recommend a deep study of the Book of Proverbs by King Solomon. Its insight and advice is so profound that if we only half followed it, we would walk a better path. They cover wisdom and folly principally.

Like a dog that returns to its vomit is a fool that repeats his folly. Proverbs 26:11

Do not answer a fool according to his folly, answer a fool as his folly deserves. Proverbs 26:4-5

If a person speaks nonsense to you, do not acquiesce or agree with his ideas or suppositions. Show him the Truth in whatever gentle way you can.[17]

Always look for sound teaching which is Bible based and sourced. The Word became flesh (Jesus) and dwelt amongst us. Be wary of man's spin on the Word.

Proverbs 4 contains a father's instruction that feels straight from the Father's heart. It is all about gaining Wisdom and Understanding and contains some of the best advice:

My son, pay attention to what I say; turn your ear to my words. Do not let them out of your sight, keep them within your heart; for they are life to those who find them and health to one's whole body. Above all else, guard your heart, for everything you do flows from it. Keep your mouth free of perversity; keep corrupt talk far from your lips. Let your eyes look straight ahead; fix your gaze directly before you. Give careful thought to the paths for your feet and be steadfast in all your ways. Do not turn to the right or the left; keep your foot from evil. Proverbs 4:20-27

God speaks to unbelievers and pagans unbeknownst to them. As we must learn, the Holy Spirit resides in all people.

Sun Tzu, author of the Art of War, a book written two thousand years ago, often used for management leadership training, wrote: Those who are skilled in combat do not become angered. Those who are skilled at winning do not become afraid. Thus the wise win before they fight while the ignorant fight to win.

Even in Buddhism there is the 'saint' Kuan Yin, the epitome of universal compassion that beats the devil monkey.

WEAPONRY

Miyamoto Musashi, a samurai warrior, in his 1643 book the Book of Five Rings wrote regarding the way of the warrior knight: That path involves constructing all sorts of weapons and understanding the various properties of the weapons. This is imperative for warriors; failure to master weaponry and comprehend the specific advantages of each weapon would seem to indicate of a cultivation in a member of a warrior house.

Our warrior house is God's house whereas Musashi's would have been that of a warlord. The same principles above apply to us as regards weaponry.

In boot-camp, we start to learn about the weaponry and firepower and ordinance that the Lord can bring to fight the enemy. Like all weaponry, it must be practiced with and studied, not used rashly or inopportunely.

WORSHIP

This is an area one could write a book on. It is such a wondrous arena and the Lord loves worship. I love Jonathan David Hesler's words on it 'Worship is giving back to God what He first gave to us... Breathing love in and breathing praise out.'[18]

The beauty about worship is that it can take so many forms.

Why do we worship?

Man was created to worship.[19] God is seeking worshipers.[20] He calls us to worship.[21] Worship will be our occupation in heaven.[22]

It is the only fitting response to the love, grace and greatness of God. The main Hebrew word for worship 'shahah' means to bow down or to do homage. The idea is to prostrate oneself in order to do homage to God. I think sometimes we forget to do homage to God.

One evening when I was at church, He said to me 'kneel' and as I knelt a force pressed my back forward to the floor and I was prostrate with my head firmly stuck to the ground. Then I heard a voice say to me "Andrew that is worship! When you head lightens and you can raise it off the ground, then you can get up.' I get it quite often now especially after I have flown banners or danced.

Sometimes He takes me even further down in deep obeisance, my head and face to the floor or just curled up in a foetal position. Whatever state, my head lies heavy on the floor and I cannot raise it until He lightens the load. It is an amazing feeling and difficult to describe.

We have to remember we are talking about worshipping the Uncreated One, who created us from dust. He knew us before time began and had plans for us then.[23]

There is no end to the types of worship. The home churches in China often worship and praise Him for hours and hours. In the western church we often pay Him lip-service, which not surprisingly, He is less than impressed by.

The three passages on Martha and Mary the two sisters and their different attitudes to worship and honouring are fascinating. Christ was very clear which he preferred. His word to Martha was loving but also chiding saying basically 'come and chill in My presence as I am not going to be around for much longer!' Martha's are much maligned incorrectly. They are 'Mary on a mission.'

The story of Martha and Mary of Bethany contains three different episodes: (ibid. Elizabeth Fletcher Women in the Bible):

1. Martha and Mary are visited by Jesus (Luke 10:38-42) Martha and Mary offered hospitality to their friend Jesus, a respected but somewhat

controversial Jewish rabbi. Mary sat and listened to him as he talked, but Martha objected to the fact that she was left with all the work. Jesus told Martha not to worry about small things, but to concentrate on what was important.

2. Martha and Mary ask for Jesus' help (John 11:1-44) Their brother Lazarus was dangerously ill, and in desperation Martha and Mary sent for Jesus. He delayed coming, and in the meantime Lazarus died. When Jesus arrived, both Martha and Mary were angry and reproached him for not coming sooner. But Martha also made an extraordinary statement of her faith in Jesus. He went to the tomb, prayed, and called to Lazarus. Lazarus came out, alive, from the tomb.

3. Mary of Bethany anoint Jesus (John 12:1-8) Martha, Mary and Lazarus gave a dinner for Jesus. During the dinner, Mary anointed Jesus with expensive perfume. Judas objected to her extravagance, but Jesus defended her action.

AN ALABASTER JAR

While Jesus was in Bethany in the home of Simon the Leper, a woman came to him with an alabaster jar of very expensive perfume, which she poured on his head as he was reclining at the table. When the disciples saw this, they were indignant.

"Why this waste?" they asked. "This perfume could have been sold at a high price and the money given to the poor." Aware of this, Jesus said to them, "Why are you bothering this woman? She has done a beautiful thing to me. The poor you will always have with you, but you will not always have me. When she poured this perfume on my body, she did it to prepare me for burial. Truly I tell you, wherever this gospel is preached throughout the world, what she has done will also be told, in memory of her." Matthew 26:6-13

So in worship this woman had handed over her dowry to Christ. This is very symbolic of the Bridegroom being gifted by the bride to be.

Boot-camp teaches us worship

The Lord loves music and songs and instruments being played and prophetic dance guided by Holy Spirit. He sees through all our pseudo worship behaviours and postures and loves to see the real heart of a human longing for Him, as He is jealous for our love.[24]

Children, I know, make Him especially happy when they worship.[25]

He rewards us with glimpses of Heaven or the Throne room. His ardent followers get to visit and encounter Him. Flying high with eagles or seeing His angels ministering. Some experiences are ecstatic. These are all privileges for those who hunger for Him and seek His Presence.

He cannot wait to pour out His love over people. Sometimes it feels like a spring rain, warm and comfortable, sometimes a waterfall, sometimes tears of joy that pour out uncontrollably. Sometimes one is blown over by a gust. Sometimes we laugh or giggle uncontrollably.

As we reach out our hands to Him, he reaches back. Sometimes intense heat or jolts of electricity burst through one. This is the Creator of earth, fire, wind and water! We are magnetically attracted to Him. We are created in His likeness.

PRAYER

This is part of the Checklist chapter later and is so important for us to understand. Boot-camp should take one through prayer.

The day we get an answer back from Him is the day we move forward at a completely new level with the Lord. It is so exciting when He speaks and so wondrous. Let us never take it for granted.

So much has been written about prayer. Thomas à Kempis (Imitatio Christi.) The imitation of Christ and his book written in the 14th century is a marvel regarding entreaty and prayer. It's simply about talking to God.

Prayer: 'Grant me, O Lord, to know what I ought to know, To love what I ought to love, To praise what delights thee most, To value what is precious in thy sight, To hate what is offensive to thee. Do not suffer me to judge according to the sight of my eyes, Nor to pass sentence according to the hearing of the ears of ignorant men; But to discern with a true judgment between things visible and spiritual, And above all, always to inquire what is the good pleasure of thy will.' Thomas a Kempis (1380-1471)

Thomas Hammerken was born in Kempen, Germany and distinguished himself as a priest, monk, and writer. His chief contribution is his manual of Christian discipleship entitled 'The Imitation of Christ.' It is well worth reading.

The less formulaic prayer is, the better.[27] He talks like us, and listens like us. (This sounds a bit arrogant!) Keep prayers short. He knows what you are about to say and what is on your mind, so you don't need to wax lyrical![28]

I listen to people in public praying and I sometimes think they love the sound of their own voices because they go rabbiting on for ages. I imagine God nodding off in the process.

The best intercession and prayer is using what He has on His mind, not ours![29] Lord, is this on your mind? 'Yes.' Well I really want to intercede for it! A key way of discerning if something is on God's heart is to see whether it lines up with the revealed Word of God, made explicit in scripture.[30]

There is the inner audible voice of God and sometimes the audible voice of God. Sometimes He sends angels to convey a message.[31] We will talk about them later. Other times our prayers are answered with visions, dreams, pictures and words.

Often He sends other people with the message to us. He can and will use any means.

THE CASE OF THE NO 23

The story of the police in Soho London is lovely. One night I went over to a group of London police officers who were changing shifts. I carried cakes to them and they asked me what we were doing over the other side of the road with our table and other stuff. I told them we were a ministry of Christian 'prayer warriors', working against the forces of evil in Soho. We worked in the spiritual, they worked in the temporal.[32] They liked this and one of them told me they kept getting the number 23. Jokingly I asked if it was the number 23 bus, knowing full well what it meant. Everywhere they looked there was the number 23. It was on pages and walls outside buildings. They were finding it a bit spooky!.

Just as I was about to answer, a colleague of theirs chipped in from the other side of the group. "It is Psalm 23, the "Lord is my shepherd!" The Lord prompted me and I shared some verses with him.

Even though I walk through the valley of the shadow of death, I will fear no evil, for you are with me; your rod and your staff, they comfort me...And even better; You prepare a table before me in the presence of my enemies. You anoint my head with oil; my cup overflows. Psalm 23:4-5

The police were stunned by the significance of what He was trying to tell them. Even the table across the way loaded with sandwiches, cakes and drink took on a greater meaning. They were indeed walking through the 'Valley of the shadow of Death' and were protected. I have told this story to many police since and it heartens them.

Here the Lord had communicated in an unorthodox manner but it was up to us to pick up the message and process it. It was fun!

Sometimes He uses digital alarm clocks for verses in the Bible for us to look at. I got woken up at the same time four days running and it was a verse from the Bible which He wanted to communicate to me.

Here are Some practical examples of boot-camp exercises.

- Keep a journal of thoughts, prayers, prophecies and words spoken by you. Put in any sketches or poems or verses that strike a cord. I use an iPad for notes and try and keep my own record of sermons, homilies or well preached words.
- Keep a note of breakthroughs or insights that have come from downloads from the Lord. Keep a note of any words of knowledge or prophetic words given to you by people to pray and dwell on. Seek confirmation.[33]
- Find time to dedicate quietly to the Holy Spirit and also a special place every day. Find music to play that facilitates one reaching 'a soaking state.' Soaking is when you are really in the Presence of the Godhead. All the rest is about getting into that 'state of rest'.
- Remember if you are 'transmitting' to Him, it is very unlikely you are 'receiving'! Stop and just 'receive'.[34]

- Wait to hear the inner audible voice. As said before, it may be externally audible too. As you draw closer to the Presence, expect to feel a major shift change in the atmosphere. Do not be afraid!
- Turn off all mobiles, buzzers and bleepers so as not to be distracted. When you go jogging or dancing, take some really special worship music that resonates with you.

There is no rulebook on the way God speaks to us, or how we should react or understand. It differs for everyone.

Although our God is an awesome God, unless He has something majorly correcting to say, He is gentle and you may feel incredible peace, warmth and love that is indescribable.

I have had many instances where my Spirit squirms when human behavior takes over from 'Holy Spirit decreed behavior'.

I have seen people start to speak what was clearly the will of God and others try to intervene and stop them. Be very cautious to judge or interrupt what might be happening.[35]

He can see this interruption as rebellion or disobedience and one will be convicted.[36] Sometimes He will lovingly give us the correction. Other times we will be brought to our knees in repentance.

The Holy Spirit gives us discernment to distinguish if it is from Him or not. If He has not already squirmed or cried out as well, ask Him if is this from the Lord? You will be told.

On the motorcycle, I sing or speak regularly in tongues. It keeps me calm and aware.[37] In worship at church, let yourself detach from the crowd and the Holy Spirit take over. He may well wish you to dance, or kneel, or lie down. Be obedient.

Boot-camp is where the Lord teaches you lack of self-awareness and a fearless spirit.[38]

Choose podcasts from people who really talk to your spirit not just because they are 'wowed' about by others.[39] Always check for biblical resonance and that it feels that it comes from the Holy Spirit. If in doubt ask Him : "Papa is this genuinely from you?"

FORGIVENESS

Forgiveness is the key to unlocking the Heavenly Door. Keep on 'sensor checking' with the Lord if you have released people who have hurt you, and those you have hurt. Do not forget to ask for clarity on whether you have really forgiven yourself! Often He will reveal that there is nothing to forgive from Him, but it is a lie from the enemy you must break agreement with.

I sincerely recommend Bethel's SOZO inner healing if one is struggling with matters. Stay away from all non-Kingdom healing and counseling arenas. Just because people say they believe in God does not mean anything. Unless they profess Jesus as the means and source of the healing and that He is their way to the Father, stay clear.[40]

Be under no illusion, white magic/spiritualism can heal ailments. The issue is that since it comes from the enemy it tends to have a sting attached. So do not be surprised if you break out with another illness.

Mel Tari in his book relates some scary lessons. I have close friends who have some harrowing stories. I ventured into acupuncture once and although there was relief in one area, an explosion happened in another area of my body. Never again would I make that error. I had to be cleansed afterwards.

Spiritual healing - which one are you using? The wrong method or the right one? Both methods can bring results. Both can heal. Both are powerful, one is all-powerful. Here is a little comparison list to check by. Guess which?

- One has a clear source and provenance that one can talk about. The other has a source that is vague, woolly and is unspoken of or uses earthly language.
- One heals permanently.[41] The other deceives and gives the impression of healing but always produces another issue.
- One can only be used for good. The other can only be used for evil.
- One comes from God via His Son Jesus Christ and the Holy Spirit – the Trinity. The other comes from satan.[42]
- One taps into Heaven only. The other taps into the spiritual realm and the power of the fallen angels.

- One works with Love and frees.[43] The other works with fear and holds captive.

Remember we are sacred vessels. New wine into new wine skins! No point in pouring New Wine into an old one. Onwards and upwards to the Army now that we have 'graduated' from boot-camp.

DECREE AND DECLARING

You will also decree a thing, and it will be established for you; And light will shine on your ways. Job 22:28 NASB

This is another weapon we are enabled to use. It needs bravery and utter faith.

REGULAR ARMY

For many are invited, but few are chosen. Matthew 22:14

One rarely goes into front line or Special Forces without spending a bit of time in the regular army. Are all churchgoers in the army? No, I do not believe so.

What are the criteria?
- To have answered the personal invitation of the Lord Jesus Christ.
- To have a willingness to enter into a relationship with Him.
- To be prepared to be 'born again' in Him.

As we have said, this invitation can arrive in a variety of ways.

What the Lord has revealed to me is that we have to believe the chains that the enemy has put on us, are already broken off by Jesus.[1] We have to have 'died to self' completely in order to be reborn in Christ. We have to truly believe in the God of today, that He heals the exterior and interior of us.

Certainly when you read the prophetic visions that Rick Joyner received from the Lord, satan's army is full of many 'Christians' with demons on their heads.

This is disturbing, but Christ Himself recognised the enemy's use of His own followers.

Jesus turned and said to Peter, "Get behind me, Satan! You are a stumbling block to me; you do not have in mind the things of God, but the things of men." Matthew 16:23

satan, is a Hebrew noun from a verb meaning primarily to, "obstruct, oppose,"

"I am the Alpha and the Omega," says the Lord God, "who is, and who was, and who is to come, the Almighty." Revelation 1:8

It is significant He starts in the present tense first so that we are always reminded He is ever present. The God of 'I AM'. In this way we can believe He remains the God of all things and especially of miracles and requests that come true.

Regular army soldiers are not on reserve or territorial. They are called up, but often hold key roles in churches administering serving, teaching, preaching. They will be in 'home groups' or 'connect groups' and will be reading the Bible and praying.

In practical terms all 'regulars' can become front line, but the Lord becomes more demanding for front line soldiers. He expects us to be observing the commandments in all cases and living a Godly life. In the regular army it is a 'sub-sonic' and not a 'supersonic' existence, which is fine for many - going at a lower speed and below the sound barrier.

Regular soldiers worship and praise, but sometimes continue to compartmentalise God. I believe regulars remain held back quite often from their full potential through some residual fears. The Lord adores them no less than His crack troops, but they may not receive the favour and abundance that they could receive. They are 'born again' and are saved.

Do they ever get to experience Hosting the Presence to overflow from? Possibly not. but they may experience the Presence from time to time.

They receive anointing that can remain untapped. They are given gifts from the Holy Spirit but are often reticent about operating in them, except when they choose to.

Here are a few questions to answer so you can check your own life:

1. How much do I let Christ into my life?

2. How much am I led or impeded by fear of man?[2]

I might have thought some time ago that God classified or stratified His people into categories of bravery and nuttiness or conservatism. But He does not.

The 'Mach 1 and Mach 2' speeds are available to all. It is a question of whether we want to 'pitch' for it. We have free will and He will never condemn us for choosing a different path to what He has for us.

I love the story of Jerame Nelson where he was given a stark choice of being a successful Christian baseball player who would be allowed to earn buckets of money that he would sow into the Kingdom. Or whether He went for the King's choice: a Ministry to Nations. Once given the choice and the Lord's preference, Jerame plumped for the unknown and untested because he had faith. Had he chosen the former he would have been able to fall back on his already developed skills and talents.

The Lord loves one to step out into the unknown and show one completely relies on Him.[3] Mel Tari in 'Like a Mighty Wind' tells how scared he got when he was pushed beyond his comfort zone.

What do we need to learn as a regular that we have not learned in boot-camp, before we go forward to front line?

HUMILITY

The mantle of humility needs to remain on us at all times. Christ convicted Rick Joyner of the absence of humility, in his book 'the Call.' Pride is forbidden.[4]

Everything that happens is all about God. We do nothing without Him.[5] All the Glory goes to Him. Everything we receive is a gift from Him. We do not have to work or strive for His love when we give Him gifts.[6]

Abel learned this, but Cain did not. The Lord loved the gift from Abel as it came from God in the first place. Cain's gift was the product of his labour. The Lord gave scant attention to this gift. We know the outcome in the Bible.

So if He gives us gifts, we must gift them back in praise and glory of Him.

That includes healing and prophetic ones too.

Once you have joined the regular army you will want to devote more and more time to the Lord's causes. 'Refresher courses' are imperative and dwelling on the Word day-by-day is very important.

FAMILY AND REGULAR ARMY

If one is at a stage of life where families are growing and one is recently married or careers are taking off, regular army is ideal.[7]

The Lord is often less demanding as He allows His children to settle down to life and nurture the offspring of their marriage, as this in itself is a most important stewardship to Him.[8] I believe that children do not belong to us, but are a gift from God. We do not 'own' them. Our role is to care for, protect, nurture and teach them in the ways of the world and of God. They are then 'set free'. That is why our love must be unconditional.

One responsibility of a regular army officer is to lovingly disciple his or her children grow up as committed Christians.[9] To do this we must be committed too and be Christ-like in behaviour and love. One reason why society has broken down in the western world is that we have totally failed in this responsibility of respecting the family unit that God created.

In 1998, 28% of UK families with children under sixteen were either fatherless or motherless (20% were recorded fatherless.) In 2009 of the UK 46% of children were born outside marriage, 6% had only sole person registration at birth. Only a small percentage of both parents lived at the same address. The UK statistics are terrifying and the USA is sadly no better.

The Lord sees as a primary objective, the discipling and care of children within Christian households. Christians focusing on this may find it a challenge to spread their wings in other areas for a season.

LEADER POTENTIAL AND ROLE MODEL

One of the problems about being a role model is that you only realise you are one when people start looking to you for advice or approval, or they start to model themselves on you. By that time it is too late to have honed the shape of how you are going to be or would have liked to be.

Generally one becomes a role model when one gets well known for something. Now if we intend to lead or excel in a particular area of life and we succeed, we will, whether we like it or not, become a role model. All fathers and mothers are role models.

Top footballers, pop divas are role models. Leading churchmen and revivalists are role models. In our arena we have a duty to be very self-conscious about our behaviour.

All our actions, talk and behaviour are watched. This is generally by persons younger than us, as well as peers. The younger ones start to model their behaviour on us. The peers look for cracks in the veneer of respectability. This is where 'talking and walking the walk' should be synonymous. Unfortunately if one has not got oneself sorted out before becoming a leader or 'well known', one risks becoming notorious!

Footballers or rugby players are forever under scrutiny and criticism due to a level of infantile antics off the pitch. Their marital relationships seem constantly under attack as they fail to get to grips with their new-found wealth and unlimited access to women, drugs and alcohol.

The female pop divas seem to suffer from the same disease. The real sadness is that there are millions of young that idolise these people and start to mirror their own behaviours on them.

As Christians, if we are single, and moving into leadership positions, we must be aware of how we conduct ourselves. If we are male, we should be courteous, gentle, polite and encouraging to our 'sisters.' We should honour them and treat them like Kingdom princesses.

Predatorial behaviour that occurs outside the Kingdom is forbidden within. Drunken or lecherous behaviour will alienate one very rapidly from Kingdom ladies.

If one is looking to bring more people in to the Kingdom, bad behaviour will only be seen as a confirmation of the bigotry and dishonesty in Christianity to unbelievers. The reverse will be true of course if one upholds correct Christian values and behaviours to the unsaved.

People are immediately impressed by correct values adhered to by young Christian soldiers. Here is where the role model plays such a key part in attracting people into Christ's church.

So what are the key features to be the right role model?

- A good listener
- Being loving
- Not quick to judge
- Underplaying oneself
- Being Servant-hearted
- Being enthusiastic
- Having a cheerful personality
- Showing humility
- Having compassion
- Being generous

SURRENDER

Finally, a word on surrender. Surrender is an alien word for us in the western world. We have not done it for some time as a country. We certainly rarely do it physically or mentally to each other even in marriage or relationships. Apart from some boxing fights and wrestling matches, it rarely happens.

We are taught to hold onto everything we can get our hands on, to accumulate wealth and possessions, and talents. We defend our own points of view, often stubbornly, even when clearly wrong. The idea of putting up a 'white flag' is an aberration.

However the Lord Jesus Christ demands it of us. No half measures. There is a guarantee of payback from Him a hundred fold, but often we do not know when or how. We have to give Him our hearts. Our souls come from Him and belong to Him. Our talents come from Him in the first place.

What is the cost of following Jesus?

Then a teacher of the law came to him and said, "Teacher, I will follow you wherever you go. "Jesus replied, "Foxes have dens and birds have nests, but the Son of Man has no place to lay his head." Another disciple said to him, "Lord, first let me go and bury my father." But Jesus told him, "Follow me, and let the dead bury their own dead." Matthew 8:19-22

Jesus answered, "If you want to be perfect, go, sell your possessions and give to the poor, and you will have treasure in heaven. Then come, follow me." Matthew 19:21

These are not light requests and might explain why so many churches today are still enslaved to the orphan spirit and are not listening or really loving Daddy.

Where there is unity and surrender to Him, there is unity in spirit with His followers as is requested in Ephesians 4:3. Where there is lack of surrender there is jealously, lack of freedom and competition. People spend most of their time correcting others or looking for fault. No amount of singing or exhorting works. It is in the 'being' of it; being prepared to give up all, friends, possessions, jobs, and wealth, to follow Him.

Who the Son sets free is free indeed! By surrendering to Him, we are freed. This is strange but true.

HONOUR

Much has been written on the culture (environment) of honour and both Bill Johnson and Danny Silk are my models for this. In terms of ministry, I am learning there are three areas of calling:
- Honouring the Holy Spirit.
- Honouring the authority under which one is working.
- Honouring the person who one is ministering to.

These often conflict and one is left with confusion. Sometimes you can be in a ministry situation and one of the following things happens.
1. The Leader does not agree with what you are doing or the timing to him is wrong.
2. The honour to the person receiving is not completed because love is not there or they risk being offended.
3. Someone ministering in a hurt state, may themselves hurt other

people.
4. Leading in a hurt state, may hurt people.

The leader should be honoured first. All authority is God given.[10] If the leader is wrong, then the Lord will correct him. Even if we do not agree with him or her, we must obey. That is honouring. Have we dishonoured the Holy Spirit? No, we have not been enabled, so it is no longer our responsibility. Did the person searched for by the Holy Spirit for ministry, miss out? Perhaps temporarily, but God solves everything.[11] If He intended you to pray with this person, you may do so at another time.

This happened to me once at a large home group when I turned quietly to pray for someone led by the Holy Spirit, was rebuked verbally and publicly by the leader and I stopped. Subsequently the man and his wife approached me later for a very good prayer session. I had honoured the leader irrespective of whether his timing, style, delivery, trust or synchronisation with the Holy Spirit was there or not. The Lord puts all actions to His good use.

Many styles operate in ministry and often sometimes the leaders do not seem to set the ground rules clearly. Perhaps they are not aware of other leadership approaches. The risk is that they may then over-react when something goes awry in their eyes. If this happens, we must continue to choose honour, submitting, accepting correction, not taking offence and simply seek to serve better next time.

Revival is messy and the Holy Ghost is out of the box all the time. If in doubt, ask the leader before launching into action. We must adjust our ministry to the environment, notwithstanding our own style and experience. Remember it is all about servant-hood.

My general rule as a leader before intervening with someone praying at what might appear an inappropriate moment to me, is to say 'Holy Spirit, is your hand on this?' I seek a simple 'Yes' or 'No'.

Finally, if you are making the approach, always honour the person by asking if you may pray with them.

THE FRONT LINE

"If we [Shadrach, Mesach and Abednego] are thrown into the blazing furnace, the God we serve is able to deliver us from it, and he will deliver us from Your Majesty's hand. But even if he does not, we want you to know, Your Majesty, that we will not serve your gods or worship the image of gold you have set up." Daniel 3:17-18

If you choose to go front line, be under no illusion that like Joseph and many other Biblical personages, people will try and 'take you out'.

What is front line in God's army? It means being in a state of readiness and heightened awareness at all times.[1] We are 'watchmen' of the Lord whether on duty or not.[2] Our radar is up and working. Receiving more than transmitting. It is tuned properly and gets rid of static where it exists.

I define it as having attained a level of freedom and fearlessness that most of the time you are impervious to attack. You sleep in your armour and battle wear. Your bible is close by you. If you carry anointing oil - in your pocket and not left at home. Handouts, flyers for your church or ministry are on you. Your worship accessories are close by. You have music for soaking, praise worship and giving thanks.

From a 'flesh' viewpoint, as an ordinary mortal of course, one will be affected by criticism and insults and insidious behaviour, jealousy, etc. The secret is to be as much in your 'spiritual body' as possible.[3] This permits the protection provided by resting in the knowledge and presence of Christ's love.[4] It allows one to 'flush' the incoming enemy barbs and missiles and not let them 'stick'.

Self-awareness, caution and care should always be taken. One does not want to be compromised, set-up or accused unjustly. Joseph made a mistake through lack of caution. Joseph had command of the whole of Potiphar's household including presumably knowing where everyone was working. He allowed himself to be alone with Potiphar's wife. Before she made her direct approach, it is not unreasonable to believe he had sensed that that she 'fancied' him. This was an oversight, it would appear. Even if he had no way of having someone nearby to refute the accusations, the story for us is a good cautionary one.

SPIRITUAL ADVISERS AND FATHERS

It is very useful to have wise and honest counsellors.[5] All warriors need male and female warriors to talk to 'bounce' problems off and gain wisdom from. In the front line, trust and brotherly love is implicit and there are no agendas. Age in the Kingdom is irrelevant. One can have a spiritual father younger than one or much older. The wisdom and love comes directly from God, so often advice given is way beyond the normal 'ken' of the giver were it not for the wisdom they have received as a gift from the Holy Spirit.[6]

There will be times when you are under major attack. Wise counsellors can be safe to talk to, pray with and receive guidance in confidentiality.[7] Choose your counsel carefully.[8]

INTERCESSIONARY PRAYER

Prayer intercessors are crucial for cover and intercession. Prayer cover by friends is similar in normal warfare to 'covering fire' as the soldier breaks out into the open. Generally one is also calling in Heavenly air support and artillery.[9]

Intercession is effectively being a 'go-between' to the Lord and praying on behalf of some matter. I like the description of going to the Throne Room and asking if some issue is on the mind of the Lord and then interceding for it. Jesus is the ultimate intercessor to His Father on our behalf.[10] Sometimes He comes to one directly and requests intercession and action, as you will see in the case of broken eggs story later.

This can be because someone or a group of people are not listening to Him or doing what they should be doing. The most powerful intercession by us mortals is praying for something that is on the Heart of the Lord. For example He abhors abortion and pornography, war, lack of love, the vulnerable being hurt.

Since God is Light and extinguishes darkness by His presence, we must always go to Him if any darkness arrives in our life. Only He can destroy it.[12]

Because God is love, we must always go to Him on issues of the heart.[13] Any ministry that is needed between males and females should be done where possible with an additional person. There should never be two men praying for a woman. 'Unhealthy soul ties' can pass.

In small church groups and among close friends, relationships may differ, but with acquaintances, the enemy always loves to throw 'hand grenades' in. Impartation and blessing is different as there is generally no ministry happening.

Orphan spirit

So much good literature has been written on this topic, I am not going to dwell on it too much. Put simply, do we really believe who our Daddy is? If we do not, we have the orphan spirit.[14]

Irrespective of how wonderful our earthly parents have been or are, nothing replaces the love and sense of belonging that is receivable from God the Father and the Trinity.

We have to feel like we are Sons and Daughters of the Most High. We are Royal and part of another Kingdom.[15] Women should feel like Princesses and be treated as such.

Men should feel like Princes and act like them. We serve the King of Kings and Lord of Lords and no one else.[16] This is the true litmus test of being a Warrior and in the Front Line.

Where there is jealousy or anger or insecurity or fear or lust etc., we are not acting like sons and daughters. There is no hate, illness, failure, anger, and lust in the Kingdom.[17] If we carry these things, we carry the world's issues not Kingdom ones.

So when we feel it in our 'born again' state it is because we are not seeking His Presence enough. We are seeking the counterfeit comforts of the flesh.

In the regular army, there is much more prevalence of mixed behaviours. God uses His people at all stages of their life whether completely repaired or still broken.[18] Many churches of today have their share of Pharisees with good intentions and bible-knowledge. Sometimes they can seek to 'over-control' prayer, prophesying and ministry through the Holy Spirit and have a genuine fear of man that manifests at all levels.[19]

In churches where the Spirit and the Word co-exist there is generally more freedom and trust. However in these ones, the enemy is forever launching all-out assaults on apostles, teachers, pastors, prophets and evangelists, as well as followers, as he sees them as a major threat.

Many churches have collapsed due to temptation, arrogance, jealousy, pride, idolatry or greed for wealth taking over.

The need today for many churches to be in secular buildings that house a variety of activities during the week, puts them especially under attack as residual 'evil' can remain in the building when a service starts.[20] Front line troops are aware of this and take precautions cleansing before services.

What services do front line troops perform?
- Ministry
- Prophecy
- Apostolic
- Preaching
- Pastoring
- Intercession

Everyone can be a leader in the Kingdom. Every one can receive a strong anointing and gifts. Gifts of healing can be found in children of nursery age all the way up to elderly people. Jesus said 'go out and heal the sick.' He did not set an age limit.

AUTHORITY

In all cases where you work in a church or group, remember to honour the authority of the person leading that church or group and work under it. Your ultimate authority is of course God to whom you are answerable.[21]

MINISTRY

As you go, proclaim this message: 'The kingdom of heaven has come near.' Heal the sick, raise the dead, and cleanse those who have leprosy, drive out demons. Freely you have received; freely give.' Matthew 10:7-9

Through Him we are given the power to do these things. Now we do not do it without Him as He is doing the healing as 'Christ in us'.[22] However some people have this as a major gift and because they use it in faith and love and obedience, often the results around them are staggering. If we are given them in abundance we must do it in humility and praise of God's power as we co- labour with Him.[23]

PROPHECY

Some front line soldiers wear the mantle or office of prophet. All of us can receive the gift of prophecy but the Lord gives some people the mantle, which they carry.24 Generally these people are in very close communion with the Throne Room, day in and day out. They receive visions and 'downloads' and act as advisors to the apostles or church leaders. One instinctively knows they are speaking with authority. They get cross confirmation from other prophets or recipients of the Word.

The Lord may interrupt a Prophet's daily activity, at any time He chooses.

They immediately become a sort of receptor of the message from the Throne Room. It is awesome to see. It is often very tiring for the person involved and they need rest and peace after, as well as needing a 'top up' of supernatural energy.[25]

They receive strategic advice from the Lord, particular actions to carry out or messages to convey to the Church. Sometimes these people are not chosen to interpret the picture or dream or words and others are given the gift of interpretation.[26]

Front line troops obey. As in the modern army, if they break ranks, it can be disastrous. If they show insubordination, or don't listen to orders clearly, the results can be catastrophic. So much depends on a unified front in the Spirit.[27]

I, therefore, the prisoner of the Lord, entreat you to walk in a manner worthy of the calling with which you have been called, with all humility and gentleness, with patience, showing forbearance to one another in love, being diligent to preserve the unity of the Spirit in the bond of peace. There is one body and one Spirit, just as also you were called in one hope of your calling; one Lord, one faith, one baptism, one God and Father of all who is over all and through all and in all. Ephesians 4:1-6

This analogy of the human body explains the nature of this unity.

> 'The human body is first, an organic unity. It consists of many parts: toes, fingers, hands, feet, legs, eyes, ears, etc. But it is not a collection of parts put together as in an automobile or as in a house. It begins from one cell, which begins to develop and to grow, and shoots off little buds that eventually make up the variegated parts. This is an organic and a living unity by creation. So is the church, 'spiritually speaking.' ibid. J Hampton Keathley III

Ironically when war-wounded lose limbs they often feel the existence still of that limb after losing it. It shows how 'spirit' we are as the cellular structure remains in the Spirit although the flesh and bones have gone.[28] This will be how we are in Heaven. The body remains on earth but the form and sense of the body in the Spirit will remain. Ian McCormack experienced this when he was taken to Hell and Heaven in 1982.

We have to be an organic and a living unit with each other as we form and create the End-time Church.

And God has appointed in the church, first apostles, second prophets, third teachers, then miracles, then gifts of healings, helps, administrations, various kinds of tongues. 1 Corinthians 12:28

APOSTOLIC

This word means 'sent out'. Jesus chose His apostles and sent them out to disciple the nations. Apostles are spiritual leaders and the supernatural link to the Godhead rather than 'church' link.[29] They work with the prophets, listening to them for guidance and strategy, seeking confirmation.

Then the eleven disciples went to Galilee, to the mountain where Jesus had told them to go. When they saw him, they worshiped him; but some doubted. Then Jesus came to them and said, "All authority in heaven and on earth has been given to me. Therefore go and make disciples of all nations, baptising them in the name of the Father and of the Son and of the Holy Spirit, and teaching them to obey everything I have commanded you. And surely I am with you always, to the very end of the age." Matthew 28:16-20

Apostles are definitely frontline troops. Two thousand years ago they lived off the generosity of believers. They gave up everything to follow in their Lord's footsteps. They went from place-to-place birthing churches and acting as spiritual fathers, discipling (teaching) the ones to follow in their footsteps. Many exist today in the same way around the world.

This is not to confuse the role with evangelist, as many apostles today are evangelists as well. Both roles require extreme bravery, ascetic lifestyle, discipline, prayer and preparation as well as long hours with the Lord.

The term evangelist has been widely used. The Gospel writers were evangelists as well as John the Baptist who heralded the new covenant and Christ's arrival. Now the original term covers 'an occasional preacher, sometimes itinerant and often preaching at meetings in the open air.'

A 'revivalist' of today is also an evangelist. An evangelist is a gift from Christ to the church. An old fashioned view of the evangelist is of someone who is an itinerant preacher. The biblical view of an evangelist is someone gifted to lead unbelievers to Christ, but also a servant who is called to equip believers in a body to be effective witnesses.

PASTORING

Pastors are around to help sort behaviour out. To guide, manage and direct their Christian flock. They are the shepherds who welcome in the lost as they enter the Church. They are the ones who the sheep, already in the fold, go to for advice and counsel.

These individuals have to be beyond reproach, well balanced, peaceful, calm and loving. They may have very likely been evangelists. They will be excellent listeners and worldly wise.

We know well that most unbelievers, when they smell religion, run a mile. Why? They look inside churches and see a few people who they cannot identify with for a start. They see over-enthusiasm to convert, false modesty, inconsistency between 'form and content' and counterfeit behaviour.

The lost 'young' peep in and see their counterparts smiling and joyous with camaraderie and eclecticism and wonder what 'substance' they are on.

They see some churches full of 'beautiful people' who praise God and sing loudly but still seem to be breaking most of the basic commandments. Sleeping with people outside marriage, drinking too much, taking narcotics, having abortions. Often the churches have as many broken family issues and divorces as the rest of the world.

What makes them good role models to unbelievers and a good reason to become followers of Christ? Not much.

Herein lies the conundrum. Front line troops learn to be good role models and they work at it. They practice celibacy until marriage, purity and humility. Are they any less open to temptation? On the contrary, they are exposed often to more.

To the normal world and its values and behaviours, they are strange, odd, eccentric, weird. However, in a funny way. they earn great respect for their 'form and content' because the 'inner life' mirrors the 'outer one.'

This new front line of young and old, once they have got over the awkwardness of wearing their faith on their sleeve, feel much happier. They will lose some close friends and feel they need to avoid certain 'old haunts' thereby receiving surprise and criticism from their non-Christian friends.

However if we are to bring Christ's love and message to Muslims, Jews, Buddhists and Atheists, we need to look like we are convincing.[30] Many of these afore mentioned belief systems are far more disciplined, consistent in their faith than we are.

I hope you have a better picture of what Front Line is about and how it differs from the 'regulars.' In the former, the resilience and inner strength of faith and belief is very strong and one's total reliance on the Lord.

In the latter, one is 'born again' but not necessarily working in the full strength of that state. The gifts are under-developed and used sparingly. There is still 'fear of man' around in pretty large proportions.

A very good chapter in Danny Silk's culture of Honour titled 'The Funnel from Heaven' explains the fivefold ministry well.

Among more advanced Warriors, the anointing can all operate within them and are called out by the Lord in given situations.

ARMOUR

We have talked about armour before. There is only one type of armour that works. The Armour of the Lord.

Kevlar and other body armours will protect the physical body under assault but not the spiritual body. Similarly, Armoured Personnel Carriers will protect troops to a greater or lesser extent in the 'flesh' but Prayer cover is the only true protection in the spiritual world.

On to Special Forces...

SPECIAL FORCES

Be strong, courageous, and firm; fear not nor be in terror before them, for it is the Lord your God Who goes with you; He will not fail you or forsake you. Deuteronomy 31:6

As in the world armies, whether they are called the SAS, Delta, SEALs, SBS (Special Boat Section), Commandos, Rangers, Paratroopers, there is a degree of mystique about those who serve in these groups.

Everyone knows these soldiers have received special training and work anonymously and undercover for the countries or organisations they represent. The training is arduous and exacting. The work they do is little known and their faces are obscured for identification and protection. They are the prime enemy focus as they represent real danger to their adversaries.

They are extremely well armed and proficient in the art of warfare, intelligence gathering, research, reconnaissance and captive or hostage rescuing and evacuation. They are very fit mentally physically and emotionally.[1] They are totally fearless and prepared to die at any moment.[2]

Can you start to see the parallels of Special Forces and their need in the Lord's army? They tend to be very lively, free, 'on fire' individuals. They align themselves with the Spirit of God. As a result they receive favour. Special Forces troops practice a Kingdom culture. They are trained to outflank the enemy.

THE ENEMY HAS RIGHTS

The enemy uses every technique to misguide people and distract them from their God-given purpose. His minions operate in many guises. The enemy acquires toeholds, footholds and strongholds in people by whatever means possible.[3] If a person demonstrates or feels anger hatred or any other negative reaction or lies, a door is opened to the enemy.

In essence the enemy is allowed to go to the Heavenly Court and plead the case to sift the saved person as evil or bad thoughts have been seen to reside in them. This permission is granted in most cases by God, especially if the evidence is irrefutable, He cannot refuse.

Unsaved persons of course have no need to be sifted as they are already in his domain to torture. Peter encountered this scary situation and received a warning from Jesus, which He did not heed.

"Simon, Simon, Satan has asked to sift you as wheat. But I have prayed for you, Simon that your faith may not fail. And when you have turned back, strengthen your brothers." But he replied, "Lord, I am ready to go with you to prison and to death." Jesus answered, "I tell you, Peter, before the rooster crows today, you will deny three times that you know me." Luke 22:31-34

This is extraordinary as Jesus was already beginning His role as intercessor for us and He knew prophetically that Peter would fail and his last words even show the need for repentance and strengthening subsequently.

Special Forces are given greater gifts and can see in day and have 'night vision'. They do not need night vision goggles. The Lord provides them with heightened intuition, signs, and searching and revealing words to guide them. As a result when something negative is around, the Warrior tends to 'flush' the reaction out of someone or the situation.[4] A person may 'manifest' in front of them. Darkness cannot hide in Light.[5] Nor can Falsehood remain hidden for long. The Truth is revealed and exposed.

Special Forces troops are highly trusted by the Lord and are interdependent on each other. They work in very small teams as a nucleus with cross-skills and support. They work via nodes and very hidden and coded connections with the centre, so enemy intelligence gathering does not expose them. They limit their conversation to a minimum and destroy any trails behind them. However, all the time there is 'back up' close at hand, if needed.

In the Lord's special forces, one of the principal 'back-ups' are angels. They carry many different roles in the Kingdom but are obedient to the Lord of Lords and generally need a request before they come in to help.[6] The exception is when a warrior is in immediate danger and he is not aware of it. In these cases, angels frequently intervene in the spirit and the earthly world to protect him or her.[7]

Special Forces warriors are very mindful of going out prepared, equipped, and cautious with a clear plan.[8] They know that when they let their guard down the 'force field' created by angels and the Holy Spirit is weakened. They need to be strong in faith, love and trust in their Lord. They need to know they do nothing without Him. The Power that they wield is His and the Authority they carry is absolute.

Their territory is often behind enemy lines. This means sometimes there is no help that close by and everyone they meet could expose them. They need to be able to distinguish friend from foe.[9]

The gift of discernment that the Holy Spirit gives them provides this weaponry and intelligence gathering. Since the enemy is disguised often as a wolf in sheep's clothing, nothing is what it seems.[10]

Christians of all types have been compromised by him to serve his purpose. The rest of the world, if unsaved, is captive to the enemy. However, there is no doubt that unbelieving people who have Kingdom principles and are kind, generous and loving, are far more difficult be taken captive by the enemy. They are as a result often friendly to warriors. The warrior has to test 'form and content'. Does the mild and polite exterior disguise hidden evils or controls by the enemy?

In Soho London one night, a location known for evil, where we minister salvation, healing and deliverance, I was watching a young man talking to some of our team by the table laden with food. He appeared intense but quite friendly. But there was something in my Spirit that worried me. As I approached him his demeanour altered completely. His face grimaced and he pointed his finger close to my face. 'I don't like you, I hate you, keep away,' he said. I whispered 'Go away satan!' whilst watching his eyes. He backed away slowly from me swearing and threatening.

A loud whistle was heard and I saw that a police officer had been watching the event. He called him over and within seconds the guy was gone. Here was an example of manifestation of evil in the person, which could not be suppressed, as it recognised the Presence.

Sadly too many Christians still carry enemy strongholds and do not recognise they are in them or on them. When they manifest in anger or frustration or start lying, they only feed the enemy with more hooks on them. This must be dealt with ministry and deliverance.

Special Forces therefore have a very wide remit over territory. Much of their opposition can come from Christians who have issues. What defines a Special Forces warrior? He or she is very free. That means the Son has set them free.

So if the Son liberates you [makes you free men], then you are really and unquestionably free. John 8:36 AMP

FREEING INDIVIDUALS

SOZO, (inner healing and deliverance ministry) is one solution. The level of ministry will depend on the individual and whether they want to be cleansed of the enemy strongholds. Sometimes when a person is strongly possessed, the deliverance can be longer and more intense. The spirits do not want to depart and if the person is cooperating with them, one needs to talk directly to the spirits and ask them to leave.

There are many deliverance-training ministries. The Lord will guide you as to which suits you.

TAKING BACK GROUPS OF PEOPLE AND PRINCIPALITIES

In these situations, the more warriors fighting alongside each other, they succeed in increasing the power against the adversity.[11] Towns, cities, buildings, edifices, locations and institutions that have hosted the enemy for years and years need breaking down in a more extreme way. Some warriors are chosen for this.

They pray and repent on behalf of peoples or locations asking for angels to be woken to fight. Anointing buildings and doing prayer walks to stamp back the ground is very effective.[12]

Authority is given to us over land to take back or bring back fruit.[13] 'Spiritual wells or gates' that need to be unblocked require committed warriors. Wells are the supernatural source of 'The River of Life'. Churches often have blocked wells and require aid to unblock and release Holy Spirit 'Dunamis' power.

I believe very much in the 'Seven Mountains" insight by Lance Wallnau, Johnny Enlow and others, that has been evolving over years concerning the devil's control at the very top of the following key mountain arenas:

- Family
- Education
- Government
- Religion
- Economy
- Celebration
- Media

This means that the enemy has placed 'puppets' leading in these arenas that are often unwittingly under his control. Since Nimrod and the King of Tyre this has been the case. We have seen recently these mountains starting to be dismantled by the Lord.

Money supply, wealth held in very few hands, can alter countries' destinies. Bigoted behaviours towards nations, people, favoured statuses, exploitation or unfairness all point to Non- Kingdom principles.

God wants these mountains to be led by Kingdom people who are righteous, obedient, fair, but also successful in their professions and skills.

Men and women who are awaiting the Lord's return and also loving on all people, especially the oppressed.

All meetings whether business, political, press or otherwise need to have the Presence hosting them. Their outcomes can be affected positively through powerful prayer warriors who declare Kingdom purpose over these events.[14] Prior or pre-emptive intercession and 24/7 prayer can avoid disagreements in meetings.

Major disasters prophesied, can be averted, delayed or stopped by prayer warrior intercession. I have many examples of weather conditions being altered by prayer warriors who declare an end to enemy hostilities.17

God never gives up on us even when we give up on Him.[17] Too many people, including Christians, have a niggling feeling that God is not always good or all-powerful or that he will 'come through'. God gets the blame for too many things that are in our control or the enemy's.[18]

Our God is a good God and a loving God. It does not mean that like a good father he doesn't discipline and correct us occasionally. However His discipline is always for reward and at such a multiplication back to us, we could never reciprocate.

SPECIAL FORCES PROPHETS

Often certain people are chosen by the Lord to receive messages that affect nations and even the world. At times, these messages are very difficult to interpret but if done so in time, warn us of impending events that can be deferred or stopped or mitigated against.

The dates are never precise as God works outside time. Some prophecies take years to happen. Others are so stark and immediate they need to be communicated very rapidly.[19] The Lord regularly gives prophets pictures of catastrophes or accidents.

He regularly gives pictures and words to people of what He wants their next strategic moves to be in their lives. He can lay down strategies for taking down dominions where a country or city may be under subjugation of evil.

Words have to be tested. The more confirmation one gets, the better.[20] Sometimes two prophets are given the same data and then confer later.

I have a close prophet friend who was getting much from God for her but was unsure if it was 'all' from Him. The best thing to do there was wait for confirmation from someone else reliable and trusted that also had a clear line to the Throne Room.

We may well ask why He does not just intervene. That would be too easy. He intervened in the Old Testament for the Israelites and believe it or not they became too complacent and dependent on the Miracles. They still continued to worship Mammon and false gods and use seers who did not work for Him.

No, we were given free will for a reason: To hunger for 'the Way'. Not to have it 'shoved down our throat' as an alternative.

We have destroyed the world following the wrong leader. Jesus was sent to redeem us, and we still do not get the message.[21] The Bible is the gateway to Eternity. Through the inspired Word by the Holy Spirit, there is only One Way: Jesus. Those who believe in no life after death or a spiritual realm will struggle with the concept, bless them. May they have revelations and encounters with Jesus Christ.

Those playing in the spiritual realm and with the wrong master should be very wary.[22] Though they are generally easier to bring to the Lord, since they accept there is a spiritual world, they need to renounce their ties to the heylel (lucifer) and his minion satan.

Sadly whether they are in brotherhoods, or secret societies, they do not realise who they are contracting to. Their education on the history of civilisation and the stories of the Pharaohs, Templars, pagan gods and their leaders are sketchy. Blood covenants signed and sworn in many brotherhoods and cults do not reveal the master. They are kept vague and all embracing.

If they do not mention the Trinity and the role of Jesus Christ as the Way the Truth and the Light, be warned, check what you have signed.[23] If it is Molech one bows to, it will mean the ancient Semitic God of the Ammonites, King, Owl or Wisdom but it is not Christ, nor the Holy Spirit![24]

All men will be judged on the final day.[25] That is all we know. There are only two places where they will go - up or down!

Ezekiel 16 is a good place to go to read about God's plan and covenant that was revoked by man and our pursuit of idols other than Him.

Some will say 'oh, that only applies to the Jews not us.' Well we are descended from the Twelve Tribes and God is the God of today yesterday and tomorrow, so what ever held true then, holds true now in terms of His feelings.[26] Man's behaviour and pursuits in worship and rules of Kingdom alignment may be tempered by God over time as He sees fit.

When He sent His Son to become man as the new Covenant and turn the Old Covenant upside down, there were still the Commandments left in.

Following the Spirit and bearing the Spirit's fruit is fulfilling these commandments as the Law 'has nothing against these'.[27] Love became the key and not service and sacrifice.[28] He was the ultimate sacrifice.[29]

Special Forces warriors hold love, forgiveness and brotherly, sisterly Kingdom values at the centre of what they do.[30] Everything is subjugated to these. This is why friendships that can take years to develop in the secular non-Kingdom world, take weeks in the Kingdom. Holy Spirit resonance (Dunamis) builds and a bond that is unbreakable of support and love will go through anything.

Special Forces soldiers have a spirit-to-Holy Spirit connection that is very strong.'Dunamis' is the world changing, dynamic force of the Holy Spirit working in and through a Christian's life.

FRONT LINE AND SPECIAL FORCES

Walk in power.

Jesus says: 'But you will receive power when the Holy Spirit comes on you; and you will be my witnesses in Jerusalem, and in all Judea and Samaria, and to the ends of the earth.' Acts 1:8

'I pray that out of his glorious riches he may strengthen you with power through his Spirit in your inner being, so that Christ may dwell in your hearts through faith' Ephesians 3:16-17

If Jesus recognised the power in Him, we need to recognise this power in us. Remember the woman with blood who touched the hem of His garment.

But Jesus said 'Someone touched Me; I know that power has gone out from Me' Luke 8:46

DELIVERANCE

As said previously, Special Forces are often involved in deliverance ministry. This is when a person is under the control of one or more spirits. Some may be familiar spirits that the person trusts and believes. There are spirits that cover the whole spectrum of negativity. Hatred, anger, frustration, envy, sloth, gluttony, fear, lust etc.[31]

This work has to be done often gently and with love and authority. We have authority over these spirits and they have no legal right of abode in these people.[32] One of the big challenges is the person who is afflicted needs to want to eject or 'evacuate' the spirits. If they are in agreement with them, the spirit feels very much at home.[33]

There are many books and courses one can go on. Randy Clarke's healing courses and Bethel 'Sozo' Inner healing courses (basic and advanced) are all excellent.

Other options are:

Freedom Prayer[34]

Theophostic Prayer ministry (TPM)[35]

Jesus Ministries[36]

All this work is done under the authority and counsel of the Holy Spirit and Jesus.[37]

The first deliverance I was ever launched into, unprepared and relatively untrained, the Lord upon my urgent request, guided me completely. Step by step, I asked the questions, He gave me the answer.

WORDS OF KNOWLEDGE

Do not be surprised that some 'wised up' Christians like to put you to the test when receiving prayer. Bless them.38 You ask them what they have on their heart to pray about and they say: 'Oh I thought you might be able to tell me what God tells you.' Smile and say, 'give me a minute'.

The Lord loves to trounce these types. You will normally get something that blows them away with shame for having challenged you and the Godhead. If you get nothing, just say so and ask them if they want to be blessed. That works every time!

Do not be taken out by criticism! Do not be surprised when you know where your 'word' comes from and a person wants to hear something else.

An example: A young man was very athletic and surfed a lot and played extreme sports. He had damaged his back, he believed beyond repair. The Holy Spirit gives you a picture of him laughing as he swims in the surf. You do not know he was a surfer nor know about his bad back.

Do you give the word to him? Of course it is encouraging! You were given the word not to sit on and mull over. That's 'soul' taking over from spirit again. That is a captive spirit on your part.

Also do not interpret it; wait if he sees it resonates. He may say, 'yes I used to be a top surfer.' Cool. 'But my back is crocked now' he adds. Well perhaps the Lord wants to heal you. How about that? Would you like to be healed? Now he might not allow you to go there. Why? Because He has the spirit of defeat and unbelief that he could be healed. So he may not like the word that much. He may say it's a bad word to his mates. You know better. Pray for revelation and that he gets delivered of these 'critters'.

LESSONS LEARNED & EXPERIENCES

He says, "Be still, and know that I am God; I will be exalted among the nations, I will be exalted in the earth." Psalm 46:10

This chapter is an encouragement to all hopefully. It shows that a complete 'nobody' (me) can receive an anointing and walk in the authority of the Lord. In all these stories and testimonies, the unfolding of events were managed by God all the way. This is why we must exalt Him every day.

I am going to relate some stories and experiences that I had a few years ago. I have no doubt there is more to come, as He loves to use us all. These are miracles or revelations that have happened to me or people close by. I find in recollection that most have happened because of prayer and spiritual hunger.

COMPANY TAX OVERDUE

I had to call the Revenue services (IRS) and prayed before, knowing full well that no more payment rescheduling would likely happen. I was broke and had no means to pay. I might be allowed two months. A Middle Eastern voice came on the line.

I was nearly tearful as I started to explain I needed more time. 'How much time would you like?' he asked. I was 'floored.' I said I reckoned I could pay it off in one year, month by month. After a pause he agreed! I now had tears rolling down my cheeks.I asked for his name in case I needed to get back touch with them again and asked if they would confirm in writing. No need he said bcauses it is done.[1]

He then told me his name was Mr Nazareth and that I could get back to me on the same number. I thanked him profusely and ended the call. A month later I called the same number and was totally surprised because no one by that name was known, but they had all terms recorded and I honoured the repayment schedule.

Angel or the Lord? It was a miracle.

THE LOST/SAVED PERSON

Whilst I was in New Christians at Hillsong, London, our role was to spot people who put their hand up at 'altar calls' when they turned to Christ. We then welcomed and took them to lunch or coffee. I had marked four out of the five in the reduced light of the theatre. I had an area of about one hundred and fifty to watch, all descending towards stage. Height was a nightmare, especially if they were short.

I knew the person was a woman and that was it. It could possibly be a lady with dark hair? I prayed 'Oh Lord I wish you would lead me to her. I have no idea what she looks like, but you do.'

As I exited with hundreds of people into the foyer rather dejected, I felt a tap on back of my head. I heard an inner voice saying, 'She is just in front of you.' In fear and embarrassment, I tapped the left shoulder of a woman in front. She turned and I asked if she had just made a decision to turn to Jesus Christ? She burst into tears and told me she had and I did not know what to do next as no one came to her. I told her that the Lord had led me to her. Wow! He is so good.

PRAYING FOR PEOPLE WHEN SOMETHING HAPPENS!

I am not sure when I started to branch out and really listen to the Lord. A couple of times at Hillsong, in an environment where these things did not normally occur, I started to get led almost on auto-pilot to people.

A large black woman was walking down the aisle in the lower area of the theatre and was hobbling with two sticks. I asked her if I could find her a chair and hesitently I asked if I could I pray for her.

She said she had a terrible chronic back pain so I asked if I could pray to release her of the pain. She agreed, so I placed my hand behind her, a short distance from her lower back, and asked for the healing heat of the Holy Spirit to take all the pain away. She felt heat in her back as the Spirit restored the back. Within a short space of time she said she felt much better. Thank you Lord. He had set up the encounter and my task was to go through the process. I was learning to respond to the inner audible voice and obey it.

The front Foyer of the Dominion Theatre is fairly large and in the right hand corner someone I knew beckoned me over. A young lady quite distraught in a mini skirt and disheveled was shaking. I introduced myself and asked what was going on. She said she felt she was under attack and scared.

I was not sure what to do next so prayed for guidance. The Lord told me she was a prostitute, so I asked if she was running from someone. I think it was her pimp. I felt prompted to ask her if she had anything on her that she did not like in her bag or anywhere. She had been given a big ring and as she pulled it out of her bag it almost looked heated in her hand. She dropped it on the ground, but not before I saw what it was; a coiled snake! I picked it up, took it ourside and dropped it in a nearby rubbish bin.

When I got back her face had changed for the better and she was sobbing softly. I prayed a protection over her and a young lady took her into the next service and sat with her. I am sure the Lord had much more work to do, but the path had been cleared. She was so loved and her captive spirit was about to be freed.

Lesson: He is always there to give guidance and He already has the master plan. We do not need to know it until He unfolds it for us. He may only give us a bit of the story only.

Another time, during the service, I was standing next to a diminutive Korean lady and I prayed quietly and privately for her to be touched by Jesus as she participated in the service. I watched out of the corner of my eye as the Holy Spirit ministered and tears started to run down her cheeks. The best moment was when she put her hand up and gave her life to Jesus. I smiled at her and blessed her myself, also in tears.

Lesson - always keep your radar up for the Lord to prod you into action.

A PALM TREE ON A DESERT ISLAND IN A STORM

This event marked me for life and gave me an understanding of Jesus's singular love and compassion for everyone who has been hurt. It taught me that He hurts when we hurt.

I was spending a weekend away with some lovely Kingdom people as a form of retreat. One of the ladies had had a very traumatic childhood and shared this with me early on. Towards the end of the weekend, two friends were praying with her and I was watching and praying remotely when the Lord told me to go over to her. He said that he wanted her to scream out anything that she had not spoken out of her anger and frustrations during her life, with whom ever, including Him. He told me I was to sit in front of her and hold her hands and represent Him while she was doing this.

I told her what I had been asked. She said she was ready. We sat down and her two friends held her shoulders and she began to speak. Her voice raised to a crescendo with invectives, swearwords and questions like 'where were you when?' It started like a small storm and suddenly I was alone in the middle of two raging emotions.

In front there was a beautiful bride who felt let down because her Bridegroom had not been there. Behind me was the Bridegroom Jesus in tears, sobbing. The pain on both sides was agonising and I started to sob too. But the most powerful revelation of all was that the pain behind me was ten times stronger than the pain in front. It was like I was being buffeted in a hurricane by winds from both sides. One was far stronger. His love was melting her and me slowly.

Eventually she stopped in exhaustion and relief as I think she understood that He had always been there and had always loved her. He asked me to hug her. I asked her if that was OK and she said 'yes'. This type of affection was something she had found difficult before to handle and she allowed me to do so and felt ok.

Lesson: Although this lovely person had been going through a journey with the Lord, His master plan for her healing was still rolling out. I did not need to know what had happened before nor what would happen after. I was part of the restoration plan that He had. All that was necessary was to be loving and obedient to His instructions.

supernatural 'defib'

That same evening an even more extraordinary event occurred. A male friend had stopped breathing and was going gray on the sofa. Without any compunction, I felt myself putting out my left arm and fingers and splayed my hand flat on the area of his heart. I had no idea how my hand got there. God did. I shouted 'come forth!' The man jolted under a massive electric shock which knocked me backwards and he started spluttering back to life.

Lesson: Follow instructions even ones that don't seem to be in your control that seem right at the time. Never question. God knows what He is doing all of the time! How do we resonate with what is on God's mind and heart? This is an on-going journey for me and I am sure for many warriors.

THE CASE OF THE BROKEN EGGS

This story displays the amazing stage management God puts into everything and where He manifestly is the Author and Finisher.[2] We are an important part of the plan, an actor on the stage who is supposed to play his part at the right time and come in on cue.

On a Monday morning in 2011, before going off to see a client, I went to the fridge to get out my customary egg, to boil or fry. As I took one, another fell on the floor.

On Wednesday morning, two fell on the floor. I am pretty dexterous and catch items well. What was happening? Did I have coordination issues arising?

On Saturday, I took out two eggs and four fell out of the tray in the fridge smashing to the floor! The mess on the floor was awful. I closed my eyes asked the Lord what was happening and was he trying to tell me something?'

Immediately I saw the letters ABORTION appear in front of me in capitals. I opened my eyes and looked down and choked as I saw the broken eggs! Within seconds I was sobbing and I cried out 'What do you want me to do?'

He told me "I want you to intercede. I am sad and angry. I want it to stop!" Now perchance, (chance does not exist in God's plans) I was off to the second day of Corey Russell's (IHOP-KC) conference in London. On arriving, although we had not met, I approached him on the way to the front, introduced myself and related the story.

Corey confirmed it was definitely from the Lord and very timely, because in America the pro-abortion and anti-abortion lobbys were battling it out that week in the House of Representatives. The legislation would allow the abortion pill to be taken without any reference to doctor or advice at home by women. Fifty million abortions have been recorded over the last thirty years in the USA. Wow.

Sunday came and a friend of mine rang to arrange to go to an afternoon service at a church in London. The time worked well as I was going on to my church later.

Towards midday she rang again to say she was unable to make that time but was I able to go to another church at a later time! This meant a conflict with my own plan to go to my church. I asked the Lord and He said to go to the different 6pm one.

So off I went to a church I do not normally attend. Hundreds of people were there, all between 18-40. They were lively, intelligent and 'go-ahead' types. In the end my friend does not make it to the service but another friend, Julia joined me and we settled down to the start of the service. Just as worship began, the worship leader got up on the stage and says that two people need to give their messages from God.

A good friend of mine surprisingly got up and in front of everyone, declared the Lord wanted all who were in a state of pain or serious guilt to come forward for prayer later. He came down from the altar and returned to join his wife. The Leader was waiting for the second person to come forward with a word and he scanned the audience.

I got a large 'supernatural' tap on the back of my head and heard the Lord ask "What are you waiting for?" Oh Lord, its me! I gingerly approached the stage and said to the young man it is a story about broken eggs. I could not think of anything more intelligent to say!

I slowly related the story of the broken eggs and there was much laughter. I got to the punch line and physically faltered and sobbed. I spoke out God's word, communicated His unhappiness and explained what we must do. Stop abortion, pray and intercede.

Audible gasps in the crowd occured and I went back to my place. At the end of the service I approached the vicar leading the service and introduced myself. He thanked me for the word and said that it was a major issue in the church today and they were struggling with the numbers of young who have had abortions. I asked whether it was one in ten, one in fifteen? He said more like one in five to one in seven! Now I knew why I had been called there! God is good and His plans will always succeed. No church is exempt from failing to speak out. This particular church is a wonderful one.

Sometimes practicality, embarrassment, current earthly religious strategies persuade leaders to hold back when the Lord wants them to stand firm and go forward.

The Lord once told Bobby Conner he was fed up with churches tiptoeing around the sensitive areas of righteousness. He wants Christians to put their heels down first, then their toes, and wherever they go take back the ground the enemy has taken.

Lesson: This was the most beautifully stage-managed event by the Lord of Lords that I have ever participated in; the stage, the actors, and the cues. Even the location and the timing were perfect. No one but God could have stage managed and master produced this.

One thing you will notice is the actors in this story learned their parts, came in on cue and were utterly obedient to instructions and timing.

What must not be forgotten is that the Lord does not condemn people. He is angry at the permissive society and the lack of moral education. He loves His daughters. They are amazing to Him. He hurts for them, irrespective of whether they had their terminations before they became Christians or became born again. There is no condemnation.

He is angry at exploitation. He is furious about manipulation and coercion. He is sad that so many lovely people find themselves in this state and are ashamed because the enemy has made them feel like outcasts. He wants reconciliation and love. Many churches do post abortion counselling, if people are not scared to come forward.

What He is looking for is preventative measures. Better education. Morally driven legislation by Government, to ensure better behaviours and standards.

THE CATALANS ON A FLIGHT TO BARCELONA

God turns up everywhere with me and will interrupt my flow of thinking, resting, dreaming or speech whenever he wants. He has every right to. He is Papa, my Daddy. For some inextricable reason, He does this when I travel through airports especially.

I know He has done this with Maggie Colvin and Jen O'Brien, two very gifted and anointed Princesses I know. Do read Maggie's book Miraculous Love about her exploits with the Lord. This can happen for you all. We just have to hunger to have encounters.

I was flying to Barcelona and reading 'Culture of Honor' by Danny Silk. The Lord suddenly started speaking to me. Engrossed as I was, I was being given a task to do. He wanted me to open up a conversation with the couple on my right and He would guide. I was to introduce myself as a Christian and ask them if they were.

So I turned and smiled to them and they smiled back. I introduced myself and went through the preamble. When I asked them if they were Christian, I was told '"certainly not, No". It was a very final statement!

Now the Lord sort of works like a drip-feed to me. Somewhat like an earpiece coming from the Director/Producer desk that newscasters have in their ears. Feeding new bits of information and guiding as you remain glazed on the lens.

"Ask them if they have children." which they did not. Next, ask them if they are looking forward to having children, which they were not.

Lord, this conversation is going rapidly in a southerly direction, I mutter to Him, wriggling in my discomfort. Then came the punch line! "Tell them I am going to bless them with children."

Pause, internal wrestle with God, "You must be joking. Can you find someone else to say this to them?" He simply replied, "No, it is you.'

Oh dear. So I launch. As you can imagine stunned faces looked back at me, and all conversation stopped. I smiled and silence came from the Throne room.

Relief. I could get back to my book.

On landing I got up first, preparing myself for a hasty departure and then lent down to say goodbye. I was faced with two broad friendly smiles and they said "thank you"!

I have no idea what had gone on between the first and the second conversation but the Lord had been at work. Phew!

A little later, in January 2011, Bobby Conner was in San Diego and gave out a decree from the Lord in the church - a breaking the spirit of barrenness and all maladies that prevent the birth of babies, endometriosis, fibroids, fallopian tubes, etc. Five women got up and were released to become fertile. Wow! I thought about the two unbelieving Catalans who would birth children decreed by the Lord.

On my flight to San Francisco from San Diego, a lady sat down next door to me. I got prompted to open a conversation with her by the Lord, although again I was immersed in my book. She turned out to be a Christian married to a top Mexican oncologist and she was an occupational therapist in hospitals. They had been married for some years and wanted a baby, but were unable to bear children.

I just knew what was coming but said nothing. He asked me to ask her about where she had lived before. 'Barcelona' she said so I told her the testimony of the Barcelona unbelievers, the decree of Bobby and then I declared an end to their striving for children, promising offspring per the Lord's instructions. That is so cool?

Lesson: God's master plan for people and places and things rolls out in His time, over time and the links sometimes only become apparent later.[3] Our task is just to do what He asks us to do. 'Thy Kingdom Come, Thy Will be done on earth as it is in Heaven.'[4]

There is fruitfulness and no illness in Heaven. He does not want it on earth. The irony of the unbelievers being able to conceive and not wanting children, the believers being unable to and being rewarded for their patience, was not lost on me.[5] I marvel at His Love.

A COUPLE FROM ZURICH

I was flying back from California into Switzerland and then to London City Airport. Seated at the front, an old couple came on board the plane and sat down in the row behind me. They looked in their early seventies and one was English, the other Swiss. They spoke quietly in French and English. Gentle and with kind faces, I just noted them as they sat down.

As usual I had a good book to read and put on my music before take-off. I glanced back over my shoulder and the lady caught my eye and smiled at me. I smiled back. Around mid-flight the Lord told me He wanted me to talk to these two people and to tell them He love them very much and they have been wonderful parents and grandparents during their lives. I was to convey this message that they are very blessed and loved. He also wanted to release the spirit of anxiety and worry from the lady that has been plaguing her for many years. Message over!

Here we go again, total strangers with a message from God. How to approach? No answer came. I was left to my own devices to choose when was the moment. Do not think even with experience one necessarily becomes more brave. It does not. One prays to host the Presence and the Lord will open the moment to approach with the right words.[6]

By the time the plane was landing, I had not worked out my strategy and was beginning to panic. I had to text my driver who was picking me up. The taxi pick up rank at the airport is a nightmare and almost like landing slots for planes on the runway.

By the time they had gone out before me and I was following them, I still had no plan. The baggage handling area appeared and I was just about to completely forget my mission when I got a jolt reminder from the Lord. "Haven't you forgotten something?"

I walked back looking for them. As I approached, the lady turned towards me and immediately grabbed both my hands like a long lost friend. This action of hers, so startled me, I jumped back a step.

"I am here under orders," I quietly said, smiling at her whilst thinking what a strange thing to open a conversation with! She would not let go of my hands. "The Lord Jesus Christ has instructed me to give you a message." Then compassion fell on me as I told them how much He loved them and honoured them for whom they were.

"Who are you?" she said. The husband looked on quizzically but also in a very friendly and humble manner. I think for a moment they thought I was an angel! "I am just God's messenger. You do not need to know my name." Remembering the final instruction, "He has asked me to release you 'Mam' of the spirit of anxiety that has hung over you for many years." I declared this over her.

I blessed them and finally she let go of my one remaining hand and as I parted I said "My name is Andrew. Good-bye." Job done. The couple thanked me profusely and I left at speed for my cab.

Now I have no knowledge of what the Lord did after that. My task was done. It felt good and it had really rocked me as I conveyed His love for them.

Lesson: Many times one will never know the answer until one arrives in Heaven. I look forward to meeting them again. Their children and grandchildren are so blessed by them. Their Papa just wanted to tell them how special they were to Him. That's all that needed to be done. He is so wonderful.

THE MAN WITH CANCER

This story is lovely as it combines so many attributes and ways that the Lord works with us and heals people.

In 2010 at an event in Tonbridge, England, a friend of mine and I were asked to minister in their healing rooms. During one of the services we were drawn to a family whom I had seen at another church. We went to say hello and it turned out the father had cancer and prayer was needed for healing. We both prayed and got words for him and moved on.

In 2011, I was at a Good Friday Service in a large church, which included a choral performance with the choir in black tie. It was a wonderful. As I was watching I closed my eyes and prayed. Suddenly my eyes saw a man in a white linen shirt at the back of the choir singing next door to a friend of mine. I opened my eyes and the man was not there. Closed them and he reappeared.

I knew my spiritual eyes were at work but never had I seen such a clear depiction. Grey hair, almost white, a white tee shirt, in his sixties. Where had I seen him before? He looked familiar. He was the man in Tonbridge! Then a voice said 'I want to heal him totally of cancer'

This was pretty tricky. Where was this man as he manifestly was not there in the choir at that moment? I searched high and low round the church. I spoke to two pastors and asked for them to keep an eye out and told them the word and vision I had seen. No luck!

Then I saw a friend of mine who has a close line to the Throne Room and asked for her to pray for me to increase my discernment. A few minutes later I was drawn towards the exit and down the steps. There, at the bottom of the steps was the daughter of the man we had prayed with over months before resembling the man I saw in the choir. This was too much of a coincidence.

I related the story and the Word and she was convinced God was talking about her father. What is more, he loved singing in church! God has a great sense of humour, remember?[7] She rang him and conveyed the message. I understand the signs of healing are very good and keep in touch with them. He was not wearing a white shirt but a green one that somewhat disappointed me.

The next morning I was sitting on my sofa and the Lord gently said to me, "Andrew, what is the colour of green supposed to represent?" Oh my Lord it's healing! I said." I burst into tears of joy. ' I am so sorry, "Thank you Lord for reassuring me." I passed this on to the family.

Lesson: Why did the Lord do it this way? I have no idea. It was great fun and a challenge.[8] Maybe the time had come. All I can tell you it is a mighty privilege to be part of the process.

But you too can be if you want. It's all about serving and hunger. I had forgotten that I had prayed for an encounter at this service at the beginning. He gave me it.

EAGLES AND ANGELS

Many people are cynical about visitations from angels and seeing in the Spirit. This is real and can be experienced by all. As a result of an experience that happened to me with 'flying' in the Spirit, I just long for the next journey.

Once at a church we were all praying in tongues and welcoming in the Holy Spirit when I saw an angel way ahead standing guard and then an eagle took off towards me from the back of the altar and flew over my head. It was so large its wingspan was approximately twenty feet. What was extraordinary was when I went up to give testimony of it, two very solid respectable and trusted people, one very prophetic, approached me later and said they had seen the same eagle! Now that is confirmation!

My first encounter with angels standing clearly was at a Gary Oates evening. He lives in Moravian Falls, North Carolina and if you want to feel angelic presence this is the place to go. Behind him, I saw his angel and two angels behind each of the worship team. They had amazing musical instruments resembling lyres and pikes. I asked Gary if he was seeing angels too and he said behind me, there were many floating up by the ceiling.

FLYING LESSONS

My great friend Jean Claude took me 'flying in the spirit' in South London. I took off and flew to Canary Wharf seeing all the topography, like Google Earth. I arrived and floated round the very tall buildings there. I saw a lady in a pink jersey but not her face. On the way back, I flew into a dove that Jesus told me was the Holy Spirit.[9] I had burst into happy tears and the picture of a hand outstretched and rainbow heart fixed in my eyes.

Next day, I was at a conference on prophetic art and saw a painting on the wall that mirrored this scene. The artist came up and asked me why I was gawping at the picture, so I told her the story.

She later came over and gave me the painting as a gift from the Lord. The next day I met the lady in the pink jersey and prayed for her. Unbelievable, yet true. He is the Master Planner.

LESSONS LEARNED & EXPERIENCES

THE DOUBLE HERNIA AND THE WARRIOR CONSULTANT

A few years ago I was due to have a hernia operation. When my consultant first scrutinised me, he found a second hernia on the left side about to erupt so quickly decided to do keyhole surgery for both. These interventions are apparently rapid but still need time to repair with painkillers, etc. My prayer team prayed for rapid healing and this happened against all odds. I was up and jumping around in forty-eight hours from the time of the surgery.

A young man half my age I met in the consulting rooms a week later, had taken five days to recover moving round very slowly, just with one hernia! However the story gets better.

As I was going for my check up one week later, the Lord told me to pray for the Consultant, especially covering him with protection. No explanation, just pray hard. At my meeting, I asked him if he was a Christian and he was. I told him I had been asked to pray and anoint him and did not know why, but would follow orders. He said that was fine.

Afterwards he then shared with me why he thought the Lord had sent me. In two days time he was going to the trauma tents in Libya as a surgeon to teach and back up the medics there, especially with regard to serious war wounds on children. The tents were right in the firing zone! God is so good to those who serve Him.

He was shipped in undercover on a fishing boat and six weeks later, the same method of exit, safe and uninjured. Médecins Sans Frontières have some amazingly brave warriors.

HEALINGS GALORE

On a mission trip to Kenya, Africa, I saw so many healings and miracles that confirmed and proved His love and role as the Healer.

Praying with a partial sighted man, his sight came back completely and a paralysed man whose left side had frozen up, was restored in minutes. So much hangs on forgiveness and repentance and once this is released all healing happens.

In London we are seeing so much healing of the most extraordinary ailments that defy reason. We know it is real, but cynics continue to accuse. Just seeing the relief in peoples' eyes and change in gait and energy shows how good our God is. Weeks later and months later these people have been transformed with their testimonies.

One of my best friend's knees was repaired instantly just after her leg had been lengthened. At a street meeting, one gentlemen whom I was led to, had massive chest blockage and bunged up sinuses. The Lord cleared them almost instantaneously, which led the wife to ask me to pray for his cataracts. I covered his eyes and prayed a rapid prayer. The cataracts went very rapidly and his eyesight was restored such that the next came I saw him, he was no longer wearing glasses!

God is good all the time and when we launch out in Faith whether we succeed or not, He is pleased and happy. Psalm 2 says He sits in the Heaven and laughs and He scoffs at His enemies.

MARATHON MAN

At the end of a fabulous service in south London, the pastor had been limping and staggering around all evening not surprisingly, as he had just run a Beachy Head Marathon in England which is all rolling hills! This was at the respectable age approaching sixty, he had completed in four hours and seven minutes.

As I was leaving the Lord took over and I declared and took authority over all his pain. I announced he would have none remaining and would sleep well, with no after effects of the gruelling run. I heard sometime later, indirectly, he had been healed instantly! If you are a runner or triathlete take this testimony for yourselves.

Take all these testimonies for yourself and any others you hear. Once declared, it is not just for one person.

CASE OF MISTAKEN IDENTITY

One day in central London, I was walking past two homeless men, sitting on the side of the pavement. One had hair that was matted and unwashed, the other wearing a hood. I felt compelled to approach them and asked if I could get them some food and perhaps pray with them. They looked up on amazement and one exclaimed 'WHAT?'

I fidgeted and looked a bit embarrassed and repeated the question, saying I worked with homeless people at Crisis and felt they might be hungry.

The 'hoody' peeled back his hood and laughed and asked me to turn round. "Do you see those ropes hanging down that big building.. Well we are absailers having a break for lunch!"

I laughed and apologised. What was amazing was what followed. The 'hoody' spoke to me in a middle class accent. "You are the nicest man I have ever met and we are very grateful for your kind offer. I will dine out on this story for years!"

So the testimony will serve and although there was no healing apparent or prayer needed, two people were touched by God's love. When it goes wrong laugh with the Lord.

HIS AMAZING GRACE

Very recently at a service one evening, a close friend of mine appeared with many of her friends in tow. As we said hello, she asked me to pray for a young Egyptian man in his late twenties. I had not noticed the most sophisticated sling on his right side from shoulder covering his entire arm. He had suffered a bad sports accident and the rotator cuff was shredded, his ligaments were badly damaged and bone chips had already been removed by an operation.

I asked him if He wanted Jesus to heal him and he did. Good start! I raised his jacket and inserted my left hand and placed it on his right shoulder to apply a Holy Spirit compress. The Lord gave me a few items to renounce off him and I declared healing of all broken and torn parts in Jesus's name.

Shortly afterwards he started looking bemused. I asked him how he felt and he said "strange". Haha! I asked if he could test it by taking off his contraption. We did this and he started to raise his arm and elbow laterally, to the vertical.

"I should not be doing this!" he muttered. He said this about three times, as he gently raised his arm. I asked him if there was a problem? 'No, that's just it.' he said. "Do you feel pain?" and he said none. "I believe you are healed" and we did a high five to the Lord with his right arm! This big guy burst into sobs of tears and we hugged.

I needed to go and join the team for the start of service but at the end He came up for prayer ministry, first in line and was still crying. I gave him a big hug and tears rolled down my cheek, as I realised something far more special than this miracle had happened.

Miriam, my friend, told me after that very morning, he had declared that his faith in God was virtually gone and he had been asking for a revelation of the manifest Presence of His God for fourteen years and not received it.

That very day, Heaven spilled all over him and he felt His Father's love for the first time. I led him through a prayer of recommitment and He went back to join his friends. What a wonderful God we have. This blew me away, with His hunger to keep all His children and He is there till the last minute. He went to his consultant after and the doctor was unable to explain anything, except wonder at the repaired shoulder! From that moment of cure, he has not had to wear the sling again. He is now fully on fire as a warrior.

Lesson: Sometimes the miracle is incidental or instrumental to change a mind-set and attitude in someone. It is a lesson that we have to cry out sometimes and show commitment and not have half-hearted faith. Salvation for someone is the greatest miracle, when they learn what a wonderful and loving God they have and what His Son did for us.

AN ENCOUNTER ON THE WAY TO BANK STATION

As I was boarding the Waterloo and City line train to Bank station, I saw a couple with their daughter and immediately was 'whacked' by emotion and compassion for them but not knowing why.

"I love them very much" The Lord whispered gently to me. I was so emotionally overcome for His love for them. I had tears in my eyes as I sat down beside them. I think the daughter had disabilities. Halfway there the train stopped and various announcements came out about the broken down train ahead.

I needed to get to a meeting and so took authority over the broken down train ahead and declared that the train would be immediately repaired.10 Then came a message saying we would have to return to Waterloo as the train ahead had died. I pressed in through prayer and two minutes later the train driver announced he had some amazingly good news. The train ahead was working now, we were on our way, and we followed it into the station. The wife looked as me as I sat there chuckling and giggling to myself.

On arriving at Bank, I approached the three of them, apologising for interrupting them, telling them I was 'under orders' and had a message from the Lord Jesus Christ. I was not sure if they were Christians, but I was to bless them and tell them that He loved them very much. They smiled broadly and the husband and wife said 'thank you very much'.

I breathed a sigh and of relief and muttered to myself "Job done, Lord" whilst tapping the husband's shoulder. Bless them Lord with more encounters.

Why did He want to love on them? I do not know, but it sure felt good to be part of it.

Lesson: Job 22:28. Decreeing is so important and powerful. Take authority, as He has given us, over the situation. The power comes from having Him manifestly inside you.[11]

And I fell at his feet to worship him. And he said unto me, See thou do it not: I am thy fellow servant, and of thy brethren that have the testimony of Jesus: worship God: for the testimony of Jesus is the spirit of prophecy. Revelation 19:10 KJV

As the testimonies of Jesus can be owned by us, so our own can pass on to others.

BODY, SOUL & SPIRIT

For the word of God is alive and active. Sharper than any double-edged sword, it penetrates even to dividing soul and spirit, joints and marrow; it judges the thoughts and attitudes of the heart. Hebrews 4:12

It is important that we look at this topic, as in order to reach wholeness we need to know what is preventing us from achieving it. Whether we join the army in the end or not; whether or not we go forward to special forces or the front line, it is imperative to understand how we need to work and what changes have to be made to our life style.

I have felt the Lord guiding me over the last weeks on this topic to build what He wants to be spoken out.

Since God is Spirit (ruach) He communicates through the spirit only. The spirit door or gate is access to the glory of God.

Look! I stand at the door and knock. If you hear my voice and open the door, I will come in, and we will share a meal together as friends. Revelation 3:20

The message is clear. The handle is on our side of this door or gate. He has no access without us permitting Him to come in.

God is spirit, and his worshipers must worship in the Spirit and in truth. John 4:24

The soul is our human portion via brain and heart and the body is the truly carnal part.

The Lord God formed man of the dust of the ground, and breathed into his nostrils the breath of life; and man became a living soul [nephesh] Genesis 2:7 KJV.

The New International Version says "man became a living being."

The following is an excerpt from Grace Communion International: The "soul" can be sad, grieved, weep, rejoice, bless the Lord, be distressed, be anxious and troubled, hate and love (Genesis 42:21; Deuteronomy 28:65; 1 Samuel 18:1; Job 30:25; Psalm 6:3; 35:9; 103:1; Jeremiah 13:17). (Interestingly, the Psalmist even speaks, in Psalm 11:5, of God's "soul" as hating wickedness.) It is associated with will as well as moral and spiritual action (Genesis 49:6; Numbers 15:27). Nephesh can stand for the full range of human needs, desires and feelings, including thought, memory and consciousness (Lamentations 3:20). Psuche is the term for soul as it would appear in the New Testament.

Do not be afraid of those who kill the body but cannot kill the soul. Rather, be afraid of the One who can destroy both soul and body in hell. Matthew 10:28

ACCESS TO THE GLORY OF GOD: FULL LOVE

Spiritual gates are Reverence, faith, hope, and worship, revelation, intuition, fear of God and prayer.

Soul gates: Conscience, reason, imagination, mind, unconscious conscious, Emotions, choice and will

Carnal body gates are: Eyes, nose, ear, mouth, feel/hands feet or sight, smell, hearing, taste and touch

The soul and body gates have to be under control of the spirit gate.

Mike Parsons has done a fabulous drawing of how this works. With his permission, I am showing it below. He originally took the teaching from

Ian Clayton who received the initial downloads from the Throne Room. He has some great CDs recorded following his forty-day fast where God downloaded the importance of connecting to the Godhead.

Gateways of the 3-Fold Nature of Man

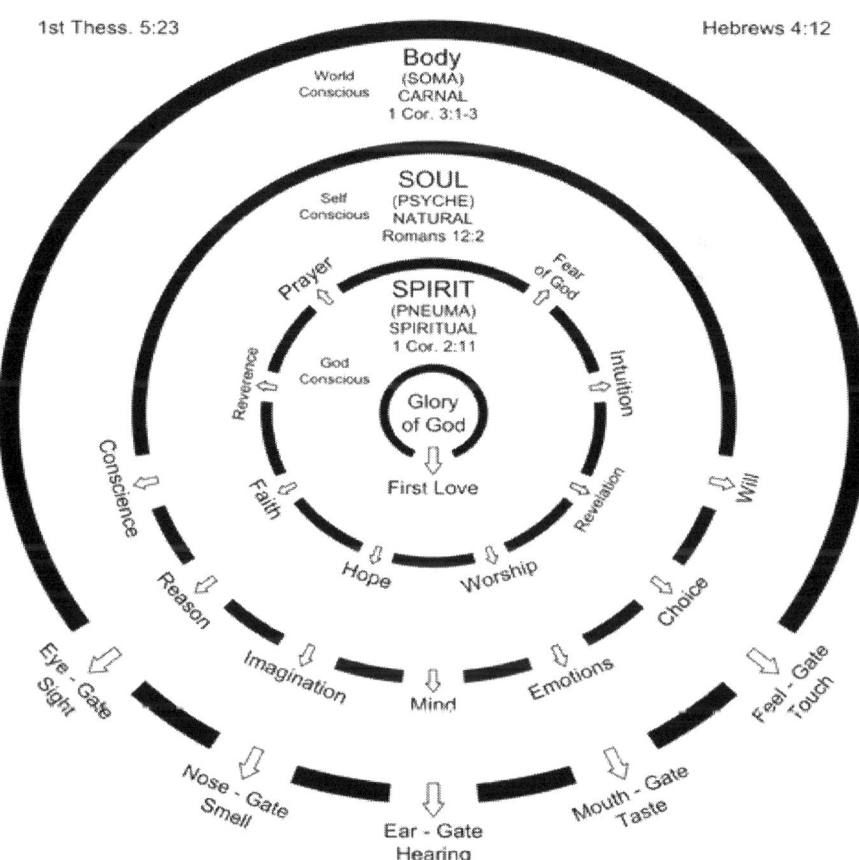

The Influence of Christ extending outward to the world

Fundamentally, we need to keep these soul gateways purified and cleansed with the blood of Jesus. The soul gates get tarnished and we cannot operate well if they are blocked. We need to take authority over these gates and get them aligned.

It is no good protecting a hurt in a gateway; it needs be full of God's Glory at all times. This is an on-going exercise. If the imagination has pictures historically of pornography, they will remain until cleansed and deleted by the blood of Jesus. When we are grumpy or down, something has not been dealt with. Ask the Holy Spirit to reveal to us what happened. The enemy loves to impact us with lies. Take ownership of the sin, bring it to the light and then paint it out with the Blood of Jesus!

A good prayer to say each morning where you hand over your 'physical' senses to your 'spirit 'senses is:

"Lord I give you my

Eyes to see from your perspective

Ears to hear Your Word

Nose to smell your sweet fragrance

Mouth to speak your Word

Hands to serve Your Purpose

I give you myself, body soul and spirit." Gary Oates

A 10 YEAR OLD IN THE THRONE ROOM

This testimony is to show you that the Gates of Heaven are open to all of us at all ages in this world well before we die.

It shows how the Holy Spirit gate works and how we can only connect to the Father through this gate. We cannot go through the Soul or Body. God is Spirit. The following is what secular people might call an 'out of body' experience. Many of us have been privileged to be taken into space or even to meet Christ or angels or Heaven. It is rare that it is recorded for posterity.

What is so wonderful here is that Michael McCormack was worshipping His Heavenly Father and his faith was so strong, he was blessed by experiencing the manifest presence of his Maker. Holy Spirit broke out and Heaven came down to take him to Heaven.

When asked to by the Lord, the 'flying experience' which I take people on from time on time, had prepared me for this event, whereas others around were not. It is rather like being ground control/co-pilot or scribe. I remain on earth, but can sense in the spirit realm and experience closely what the person is going through. It is like a sort of protector or wingman. Watching their backs, making sure they are safe from incoming nonsense.

I was at Kingsgate Church and saw Michael lying back against his chair, whimpering, but at peace. Barbara and Clare were on either side and Clare asked me what was happening. At that moment the Lord told me He was taking him to the Throne Room. They both got up and I sat down beside him and talked quietly to him, telling him what I was going to do as his co-pilot. He knew and trusted me.

The following is a transcription made by me as I journeyed on earth with Michael in the Heavenlies. As he travelled and experienced the events, I asked what he saw, felt, heard and sensed. Ian and Jane that next morning when they returned with their son, pulled out other pictures that I had not managed to transcribe. It is a living testimony and amazing what the Lord revealed to him.

A few weeks later on, Michael shared the testimony with the church on Sunday night, 10th April, 2011. These are Michael's own unedited words:

As I came into church I needed to sit down and pray to Jesus. As I did a light shone on me and with that light came an overflowing love. I was then lifted up into the heavens in this white light.

I saw angels coming around me, surrounding me as I went up. They were clothed in white robes and had shining faces with wings. They were floating around me like they were hovering, their wings were fully open and moving quite slowly and they had no shoes on.

Then Jesus was suddenly next to me in white shining clothing, and I saw the shape of His face which was light. I couldn't see the colour of His eyes or hair. His face was in this golden Light. He was twice the size of me. Jesus smiled at me and I felt loved.

He showed me Heavens Gate, it was Golden, with a massive palace & town. The palace and the town was surrounded by a wall, it was golden in colour. I then saw these massive golden gates open towards me, and I saw a bright shining light, coming out as the doors opened. God's voice spoke to me from inside. He said "Come my son." It was a voice not an impression. I felt excited about what it was going to be like inside and if I was actually going to go inside at all.

Jesus took me around lovely meadows surrounded by animals, rabbits, deer, foxes. I also saw a pheasant and a dog that was lying down and resting. Jesus took me to a throne room, it had golden pillars and paintings like you see in old churches and jewels everywhere. The windows in the throne room were in the shape of diamonds and they formed pictures, some had angels in them. The throne room was massive and there were jewels in the pillars & jewels in the walls but not on the floor. I was blown out when I saw it.

I saw two rows of angels with banners on the end of golden trumpets; they were standing in rows in front of the throne. As we walked towards the throne the angels were on either side of Jesus and myself. Their golden trumpets were raised. We walked right up to the throne and they were playing, and there were people with harps in the background and there was music as we entered the throne room.

The banners on the trumpets were purple and golden with no picture on them. The trumpets were long like they have in Narnia when they crowned Edmund, Peter, Susan & Lucy at Cair Paravel.

The angels were a bit bigger than Jesus and they had different faces. They were wearing white robes and had wings coming out of their back but their wings were all folded down.

There were creatures around the throne. They were not like real animals but a combination of different animals, like an Eagle and a Lion. They had Eagles wings coming out of the Lions backs. And they were singing "Hosanna." They were playing with Harps and some thing that looked like a tambourine {e.g. small drum with small cymbals}

Jesus held out a staff in His hand. It was wooden like a shepherd's staff. I saw three thrones. The one in the middle was for the Father. Jesus was to sit on the right hand side of the Father and the Holy Spirit on the left hand side.

As I looked at each throne, they almost looked liked they were joined together, as if they were one throne. The thrones were golden and I saw jewels covering the Thrones. The jewels were all the colours: emerald, ruby, sapphire blue, yellow, purple, plus ones I had never seen before.

The thrones were empty. No one was on the thrones and there was no one else around except me and Jesus, the angels and the lion with the wings. I looked up and saw no roof above the throne's. I saw clouds above the throne like the Northern Lights but much greater, with angels dancing in the clouds in a line.

I was taken up into these clouds and began to dance with the Angels. I felt lots of energy, hyper and the angels had instruments and there was music but the angels I was dancing with were not singing, it was coming from somewhere else.

Then the Lord took me outside to the town, it changed instantly, one minute I was in one place and the next I was in another place in an instant. And the town was lined with golden roads.

I came to a river (River of Life). It was crystal clear, fast flowing and it was coming out from the tree (Tree of Life) like a big strong oak tree and it had a thick trunk. The water was flowing from the Tree of Life into the houses and it was powering them, giving them light. Jesus dipped His hands into the River of Life and began to pour water over my head. It was nicer than real water, it felt so good! It felt refreshing and it gave me a good feeling, like after you have done something really good.

The Tree of Life had loads of fruit on it and each day the youngest child came and took a piece of fruit to share it with their families. They lived on that fruit for the day. There was different fruit on the tree and they looked like pomegranates/apples and there were grapes, oranges, bananas; every single type of fruit on the same tree.

I saw some adults with children walking down the street with their children and their faces were full of light and they seemed to be always smiling. They were people who had died and gone to heaven. Some were like toddlers, and some were like my age ten to twelve year olds; all different ages. And the parents helped the toddlers by lifting them up to pick the fruit off the tree of life. They lived in families.

The houses they lived in were plain and simple but the bricks were golden. Then Jesus took me to a door. It was a normal door and it was made from an oak tree. There was a jewel on the end of the handle. It was a Ruby. I could tell that it was a ruby as I have read a book about gems and someone had brought some jewellery to school. And I had watched a jewellery programme with dad on TV, when he was trying to buy mum a present.

The oak door opened and I went through this door and came into a beautiful garden which was the New Earth. As I went in through this door, it was covered with wildlife, lakes, waterfalls, rainbows, animals drinking from the lake and they were mostly deer.

Then Jesus said to me "This is the New Earth which we will Treasure" Jesus's voice sounded like my thoughts. His mouth moved but I heard it in my mind/thoughts; it was a familiar voice. I think I have been hearing His voice all my life, I just thought they were my own thoughts but now I realise that He has been speaking to me for ages.

Then Jesus took me out into space. I didn't see myself floating in space but I felt I was looking to earth from this space like satellite vision and Jesus showed me the Old Earth and it was covered and surrounded by a black mist of sin. I just knew it was sin. It was obvious to me as I have read my children's bible many times. What else could it be, I thought?!

The Lord then took me down to visit it and all the buildings were crumbled and destroyed. There was no life in it at all; all the plants had died. I saw no people on it; it was all deserted. Jesus said to me "This is the earth that man has destroyed. What I have shown you, I want more people to see. I have shown you this because I want you to tell the people that you have seen this and that they should turn back to God. This is what is going to happen and you can't stop this but You can help Save more People."

Jesus left and I woke up again back in my seat in church.

From Ian & Jane McCormack:

This is every parents' dream that the Lord would take their children and show them His Heavenly Kingdom. We know our son and this is a totally genuine experience. It was incredible to see this happen to him, but at times during the encounter it was somewhat fearful as I could see the Fear & Awe of the Lord upon Michael's little face. We feel that the Lord has commissioned Michael that very night before our eyes.

And last night at church before he spoke, Michael shared with me that he was hoping that at least fifty percent of the people in church would not be Christians so they could hear his message and be saved.

One point to remember about these types of experiences is that the enemy does not want it to happen on any account and he will launch attacks with any weaponry he can muster.

In this instance, an attack came from an unexpected quarter, during the journey Michael was on. Only I was aware of what was happening but I felt something was trying to take Michael out and bring him back prematurely to earth. I heard a well-meaning parishioner yelling in tongues and trying to wake him up.

It was the first time I had been given the authority. The Lord gave me a massive sword that appeared in my hands and I slashed from top to bottom, to cut off the incoming fire. Only one blow was necessary and peace returned. Whatever it was that had emerged in the atmosphere, it was stopped.

Lesson: 'Enemy Stuff' can hang on well meaning anointed and temporarily captive Christians. Be aware. This is where discernment is so important to hone.

Recently, I saw a well-respected pastor and sensed in the spirit an ungodly occult attack coming in at him, as he started to address his church. He took the precaution to declare, rebuke and cover his back with his prophetic wife who stood behind him. I had sensed something in the atmosphere and the Lord called me out for my task. That was flying banners, which I did, gold then red. I had not been asked to tell the pastor. Always be obedient to what you are told to do. My task was to impact the atmosphere.

RIVER OF LIFE OR RIVER OF GOD'S PRESENCE

The river of life flows out of Heaven. Ezekiel's vision is the key to understand what this is about. If you doubt flying in the spirit, see what happened to Ezekiel!

A cubit is the length of a forearm from tip of middle finger to the elbow. Between 17-22 inches or approximately 50 centimetres.

There is a good article to read on this at:

www.riversofjoy.org/resources_view.php?article_id=1

Jesus shows Ezekiel this river. He probably did not understand the import of what was being said.

"For I tell you the truth, many prophets and righteous men longed to see what you see but did not see it, and to hear what you hear but did not hear it." Matthew 13:17

In the last days there is to be a massive outpouring of the Holy Spirit. The River of Life, which flows from the temple at the east end, was a trickle. It was going to build into a torrent.

The man brought me back to the entrance to the temple, and I saw water coming out from under the threshold of the temple toward the east (for the temple faced east). The water was coming down from under the south side of the temple, south of the altar. He then brought me out through the north gate and led me around the outside to the outer gate facing east, and the water was trickling from the south side. As the man went eastward with a measuring line in his hand, he measured off a thousand cubits and then led me through water that was ankle-deep. He measured off another thousand cubits and led me through water that was knee-deep. He measured off

another thousand and led me through water that was up to the waist. He measured off another thousand, but now it was a river that I could not cross, because the water had risen and was deep enough to swim in—a river that no one could cross. He asked me, "Son of man, do you see this?" Then he led me back to the bank of the river. When I arrived there, I saw a great number of trees on each side of the river. He said to me, "This water flows toward the eastern region and goes down into the Arabah, where it enters the Dead Sea. When it empties into the sea, the salty water there becomes fresh. Swarms of living creatures will live wherever the river flows. There will be large numbers of fish, because this water flows there and makes the salt water fresh; so where the river flows everything will live. Fishermen will stand along the shore; from En Gedi to En Eglaim there will be places for spreading nets. The fish will be of many kinds—like the fish of the Mediterranean Sea. But the swamps and marshes will not become fresh; they will be left for salt. Fruit trees of all kinds will grow on both banks of the river. Their leaves will not wither, nor will their fruit fail. Every month they will bear fruit, because the water from the sanctuary flows to them. Their fruit will serve for food and their leaves for healing." Ezekiel 47 1-12

What does this mean? Well, we as warriors need to learn how to swim because we are going into the 'deep' and probably underwater. The fish are in the water and are waiting to be caught!

FISHERS OF MEN

Why did Jesus call them fishers of men when they were fishermen? We need to bathe in this river as it flows from the Godhead.

God has bestowed many gifts and words on me. One thing recently is a pouch with flies in it! Why have I been given special flies? In order to catch different types of fish, in different countries and places and bring them into the Kingdom. Any good fly-fisherman knows that the fly size and colour act as bait, and an attractor. Different weather conditions, different eating habits for the fish and diet, make it impossible to use one fly. The fly colours use all the colours of the rainbow, surprise surprise!

We need to wade in many instances where the backdrops are difficult to cast the fly. Scuba divers need to go catch their fish.

This river is the Water of the Word. Crystal clear and pure. It springs from wells. Hence the parables Jesus uses with the Samaritan woman at the well. The rivers mentioned in the Bible all display the power and enablement given by God when we stay in the River.

In the river of God's Presence we receive protection, love, releasing of signs and wonders, satisfaction of our thirst, miracles, a place of provision, clarification of His boundaries of authority. We receive strategy for defeating the enemy and his weaknesses. We learn what is pleasing to Him. It is where we can hear His voice. Where His peace is revealed to us and we start to flow like a river. Where our eyes are opened to people who do not know Him. Where we receive spiritual food and get re-baptised again and again. Where we will see Him in sovereign control of all. It is a place of rest and refuge. Where we will see His light. Where we will learn to rule and reign in Heavenly places. (credit to Geannine Rodriguez)

Jesus answered, "Everyone who drinks this water will be thirsty again, but whoever drinks the water I give them will never thirst. Indeed, the water I give them will become in them a spring of water welling up to eternal life." John 4:13-14 NIV

Remember the Pool of Bethesda that the angel stirred and brought healing. We can live going into the Presence. We need to swallow this water and let it flow through us and out of us. Just as we need wells in our churches, we need to be walking wells that bring forth this water of life.

Does that make sense? That is hosting the Presence. We need to leak out from every pore in our body so that people can sense it and taste it too.

That is why we sometimes need topping up, if our well runs dry. Get back in the river. That is why we work best out of the overflow in us. We need to be dripping anointing. We need to fill ourselves with this water as it is constantly flowing. It is not a lake or a stagnant pond. As Jesus said:

"Whoever believes in me, as the Scripture has said, streams of living water will flow from within him." John 7:38

Being filled with the river of God, cannot help bringing fruit and miracles and healings. As Miranda Nelson said recently: 'The water of the word becomes the wine in our lives.'

That is why it is new wine and not old wine. That is why it has to be in a new wine skin, not an old one.

I remember one day at a chapel in London where there is a deep spiritual well, Ian McCormack and I laid ourselves out on this cloth sheet that had fishes and river flow sewn into it and 'prophetically' put ourselves into the river. We were both immediately transported into the presence of God and were given different pictures.

This worked because spirit, soul and body were in the correct alignment. The Spirit was in control as it should be.

IT IS HARVEST TIME FOR US

We must reap what we have sown years back and also what others have sowed for us. We continue to sow too but the priority is reaping the harvest. It is ripe and ready to pluck. The fishes are rushing to be caught.

"I sent you to reap that for which you did not labour. Others have laboured, and you have entered into their labour." John 4:38

Tree of Life or Tree of Knowledge of Good and Evil? Which Tree do you idolise? Read Genesis 3. Are you a 'Tree of Life person' or the other one? Do you still feel innocent, not able to be offended, and capable of turning the other cheek? Good.

Are you judgemental, without enough joy and quoting too much of the Bible to justify your ways and thoughts? Hmmm. satan fooled Adam and Eve in to believing they would become more godlike with knowledge i.e encouraging them to be more Godly. The serpent persuaded them they could recognise evil and therefore know how to judge and rid themselves of it, through knowledge. They could not have been more Godlike if they tried in their former state, living off the Tree of Life.

Beware the religious spirit that started at the Fall, as it feeds off the wrong tree. The Bible is the Book of Life but Jesus is the Tree of Life, the Bread of Life and the Water of Life all rolled into one.

Jesus's followers struggled to get His message because they kept on looking through the wrong pair of glasses. Change the prescription!

'It began on a Tree and ended on a Tree. It began in a Garden and ended in a Garden' ibid. Jake Hamilton.

SURFING THE HOLY SPIRIT - IN HIS POWER

Recently, I was given my last revelation for the book. It was a picture of me on a Lillo, in big waves with surf building and crashing on the shore. I was in a place of rest but the Holy Spirit was describing Himself. I then started to surf with God, leading.

The surfing we need to learn as servant-leaders in the Body of Christ, is how to recognise, catch and surf the wave of the Holy Spirit in our lives, churches and communities.

Everything in life follows lows and highs and build and release. The perfect wave is the Holy Spirit as when we ride Him, we need to do nothing but hang on and go with the flow. The power builds up and the release is immense. The release of the power is phenomenal and awe inspiring.

If you listen to surfers talking, they will talk about being on the edge, almost out of control and yet safe. They have positioned themselves perfectly for the wave. It requires immense respect for the power of the water and the surge but also once on, riding, the momentum is created. No more need to push or strive; no need to look back and no need to fear. One is free and flying.

So it is, operating with the Holy Spirit. When we strive or do not conserve our energy, we exhaust ourselves quickly.

A surfer once he comes off the board goes into the cauldron of swirling water flow, survives by relaxing and resting and going deeper. When you wait for the wave to build you are also resting.

It is the same with the dunamis power of God. We learn to go and rest in Him, the river flow of life from the Tree. If you get swept down into a torrential river, you survive by not fighting and floating.

So it is with the Spirit of God. You take the risk to trust Him. You go with the flow. The adrenalin rush is amazing. You love and respect Him. He loves you. You hang on for dear life sometimes. He surprises you, as will the size of the waves.

Waves come in all sizes, are unpredictable and behave differently. So does the Holy Spirit! I am just getting on my new Wave.

THE SUNFLOWER OR SONFLOWER

While in a prayer soak with friends, I was given the image form the Lord of a sunflower. Its big fiery petals depicted the heat and light of the Son and the centre in brown depicted peace calm and humility.

This flower during its growth phase tracks the position of the Sun or Son. As it matures it settles down to facing the east, the source and direction of the rising of the Sun.

The lesson I received is that we must face and follow our Lord every step of the way focusing on His Light and in this way, any darkness that tries to obscure us or our path, is blotted out.

I bless you all with revelations and encounters and insight with Jesus Christ, from this book. Whatever stage you are at; novice, apostle, prophet, teacher, pastor, evangelist, businessman, or prayer warrior, I know that the Lord will have spoken to you as you read this book and manual.

The Lord wants the front line of His army to stand steady and not break ranks. You are called.

Bill Johnson summarised recently Bethel Church's mission statement:

'God is Good.

Nothing is impossible.

Everything was accomplished at the Cross.

Every person is significant.'

A LITTLE QUESTIONNAIRE

Which side of the Cross are you living on?

Wrong side: Oh Lord rend the Heavens.

Right side: It's there, we are in Open Heaven.

Wrong: we need revival.

Right: we are revival.

Wrong: we need to ask for healing.

Right: we don't need to ask Him for something he enabled and told us to do.

Wrong: worship Christ on the Cross and journey towards the Cross.

Right: journey from the Cross and worship the Risen Jesus. Spirit of Christ Risen from the dead lives in me.

Wrong: we are dead and sinful.

Right: We are dead to sin and have permission to lead a supernatural lifestyle.

Wrong: we are orphans and need to ask and have no inheritance. We need to beg like Oliver.

Right: We are sons of God and have access to our Father and Brother's inheritance. We can have Dad's last beer in the fridge.

Wrong: Struggle for righteousness. Righteous Doing.

Right: I am righteous through Christ. No need to strive for it. Righteous standing. If we got righteousness through the Old Law, Jesus's death would have been in vain.

Wrong: I have to perform to be forgiven.

Right: It's through Grace and justification I am forgiven.
Wrong: I am sin conscious.
Right: I am God and Christ conscious. This breaks the power of sin over my life.
Wrong: I fight for victory.
Right: I fight from a position of victory and favour.
Wrong: I need to fight the enemy every day.
Right: enemy has been defeated. Don't need to get drawn into a fight. Power of darkness goes when Light and Love turns up. We are Light. And Love.
Wrong: I need to work for His love.
Right: I work from Love. He can't love me anymore than he does already.
Wrong: I touch an Aids (leper) victim and get sick.
Right: I touch an Aids victim and they get whole.
Wrong: I need to punish myself.
Right: I am unpunishable. The price He paid on the Cross punished all past present and future sins.
Wrong: Human effort is paramount.
Right; I am empowered by Grace. He who abides (rests) in me bears much fruit. John 15:5.

Wrong: Life is Hard.
Right: Life is impossible! That's why I need to lean into His grace then it all becomes easy.
Wrong: It's me that lives.
Right: Its Christ that lives in me, the hope of Glory.
Wrong: Come into His presence with fear.
Right: The veil is torn. Come boldly into His Presence. He is our Father.
(Chris Gore - 'From the Hem of His Garment')
I would like to finish by giving you a priestly blessing.

The Lord bless you and keep you; the Lord make his face shine on you and be gracious to you; the Lord turn his face toward you and give you peace. Numbers 6:24-26

I pray you learn to recognise the Master's touch, to have Him prick your heart and activate and release a declaration of His Goodness wherever you may go.

If you feel to renew your marriage vows with the Lord and re commit yourself to Him:

'Jesus, you are the Way the Truth and the Light. Forgive me for straying off the plumb line and your compass bearing. I re-align myself with your Purpose and surrender myself unconditionally to you. I accept your love protection and Eternal Life. I love you so much as You do me. I commit to Hosting your Presence every day of my life and bringing Your Love to others. Amen'

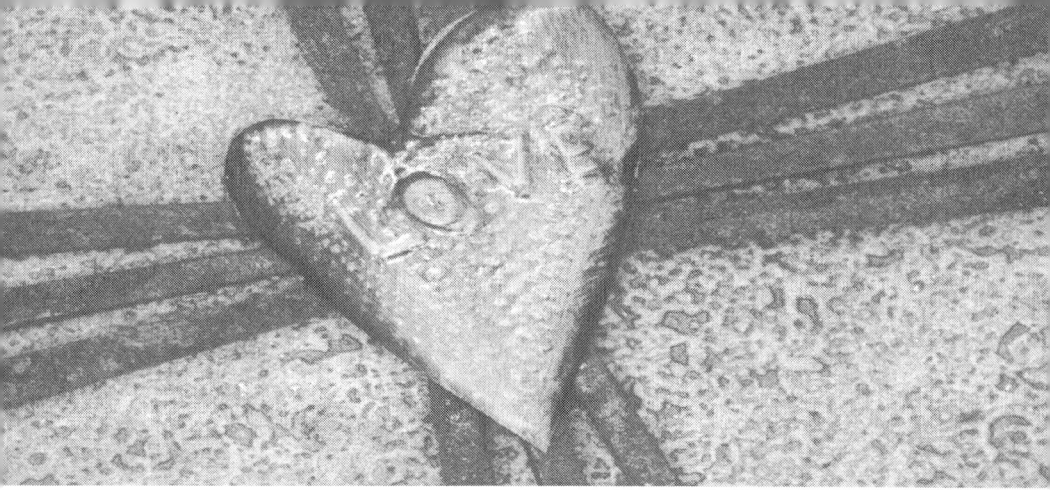

OUR AMAZING STORY

ELO MEYRICK

8th May 2013, 12:43pm, South Africa

My beloved Andrew and I were both joined in the Spirit as we were talking on the phone. Suddenly I went into a vision and what I saw was so beautiful. I saw the ancient Hebrew letters written in the air – as if it was the anatomy or the atoms of existence.

I then described to him what I saw over a message on Facebook. Both he and I got blasted enough so that we fell off the surfaces we were sitting on; me on my bed in my room and him his chair in his office in the UK.

We were taken up into Heaven where we found ourselves in what appeared to be the Holy of Holies or like an anti-room to a bedroom, where we saw Jesus sitting on a comfortable throne on the right. We saw the Ark of the Covenant as well as the Mercy Seat on top and a Menorah and gold writing on the wall. An eagle was perched on the left on a golden stand.

The Lord Jesus arose from where He was sitting on the right. He was in white with a sash in purple and a belt of gold. We were mesmerised by His sandals, and a very bright ring on His wedding ring finger. Blue purplish pulsing light jewel.

While writing up the testimony we were given Revelation 1:13: and in the midst of the seven lampstands One like the Son of Man, clothed with a garment down to the feet and girded about the chest with a golden band.

The Lord came towards us. We were at one moment standing gawping and the next we were on our knees.

My darling and I both got our individual scrolls of a golden shade from the Lord. He was given a belt – black and blue on either half and the robe of a king which was dark blue in colour.

An eagle came to sit on his right side and a dove on his left. The meaning of this being he's an eagle in the Spirit and the dove (symbolic of the Holy Spirit) will refine and perfect his human nature.

After my crowning ceremony in which I received a golden sceptre, a crown and a brilliant white gown and a blood red robe, both he and I were blasted to the ground.

We were still flat on our faces when Jesus approached us later. After remaining there for just a while, gazing at His feet and beauty, He helped us up and placed both of our hands in each other's wrapping something round them and then His hands. Both being too taken aback by all of this to realise the sudden meaning of it all: we were being married!

He then asked us did we wish to stay a while longer to which I don't quite remember what my reply was, but Andrew said 'Yes'.

We were taken flying over to a mosque here in South Africa and we both asked the Lord: "What do you want us to do?" He told us to light the mosque with His Presence and drive out any and all demons that were there. We were told to do so in that same temple's uppermost chamber.

After having done that, we saw the entire building burning with fire. His fire. Our task was complete.

Then we were taken flying further. Over fields of green with our Saviour and His squadron of angels being our protection. Being a carefree soul, I turned on my back and just spread out my arms. Andrew called out that He saw a massive wall ahead and turrets and a wide parapet. There was a cannon on the battlements. We landed there and Jesus appeared. We asked why were we there. It was the Citadel at Jerusalem.

He replied. 'Look out beyond'. We looked out and saw a beautiful countryside. (The new Jerusalem?) He then said "You are my Watchmen"

He showed us our home in Heaven and we entered it. It was a log cabin style. There was water with a lake nearby. We needed sun glasses. It was so bright!

As we were both trying to get up from the floors in South Africa and the UK, I said "Do you know what has just happened? We have been married! It is sovereign"

Andrew said I have not even proposed to you yet! He proposed and I accepted!

A couple of days later Andrew was spoken to at 2:22am and told by Jesus that the prophesy and vision he had been given some time back was complete that He would be presented with His Bride and not go searching any longer!

That word came in a Lie Bust session (a Sozo style ministry) with Brian Trueman. Brian saw a vision in the spirit of Andrew on a charger as 'Warrior of Love' with regiment of angels behind him. A lone rider on a black horse came alongside him in armour and veil and long hair with visor. He could not see the face. This was His bride being presented.

The Lord gave us Genesis 2:22: *Then the rib which the Lord God had taken from man He made into a woman, and He brought her to the man.*

AFTERMATH A FEW WEEKS LATER

We asked Papa about where and when to marry. He had been talking to Elo about the Feast of the Tabernacles for a while. We both got blasted as word Sukkhot came through and it became clear that this was the intended period for the marriage (18th to 25th September). We asked for the year and He said this year, 2013. So we asked about the day..

Elo was given Esther 5:1-3 which gave us the day to calculate from Hebrew. He gave her number 21. (It was three days after the 21st September which was the length of fast that Esther had already completed and when she went to the King. She requested that Haman be invited to dinner. He was planning the destruction of the Jews. We believe we should fast for three days before the wedding on behalf of Israel. We asked the location.

He said: 'Israel'. Then we got Galilee in the hills or down at the lake by Capernaum.

Elo was given Matthew 4:18: (Andrew's names are Peter and Andrew)

And Jesus, walking by the Sea of Galilee, saw two brothers, Simon called Peter, and Andrew his brother, casting a net into the sea; for they were fishermen. Then He said to them, "Follow Me, and I will make you fishers of men." They immediately left their nets and followed Him.

On the same day Andrew was praying with Brian who very firmly got Galilee too.

That is all we recollect at present. We are still both wrecked each time we remember this! Thank you Papa and Jesus and Holy Spirit!

POSTSCRIPT

Andrew did go to a Tabernacles celebration but at Dudley not in Israel. We encountered opposition in getting Elo's visa to Cyprus for the civil wedding. The Lord showed us a picture of us on a boat to Cyprus and adverse winds were slowing the progress. He took command of the weather and blew us back on course putting a banner of love round the ship. The next day the visa after three attempts was released to us early morning in Pretoria.

We had our civil ceremony on the 9th October in Nicosia, Cyprus under perfect skies and heat. The Cypriot staff were delightful and it was a very emotional affair. We then set off for Israel.

We arrived in Israel with a new date, 16th October, and arranged for the earthly celebration to be held on a fishing boat called Faith, by Capernaum on the Lake of Galilee. We had the Messianic Seven Blessings prayed over us

Vows on the Lake of Galilee

It was an amazing event with much angelic presence as well as the cloud of witnesses and the Lord turned up too. Very close friends came as well. We were able to plan a tour with guides and visited the Holy Land and had many encounters wherever we went……

JESUS THE MESSIAH - A FOLLOW ON

A fresh revelation came at 4:44am about rhe garment of Righteousness; the price paid for our inheritance in Christ.

When the high priest rent his robes refusing and denouncing Jesus, he detached the whole Jewish race from God. The only other robe not torn that day was Jesus's seamless outer garment. They cast lots for it. It represented the unity of the church.

The Lord just told us that the reason why His garment was not torn was because nothing could stop His garment from covering the nakedness of the people. He hung naked on the cross so that we could put on the righteousness of God.

He took us to Matthew 1:1 *The genealogy of Jesus the Messiah. The record of the genealogy of Jesus the Messiah, the son of David, the son of Abraham:*

At the first line of the New Testament the gospel writer affirms Jesus as the Messiah. This must stick in the craw of the Jews, whose Messiah He is supposed to be.

Then Moses said to Aaron and to his sons Eleazar and Ithamar, "Do not uncover your heads nor tear your clothes, so that you will not die and that He will not become wrathful against all the congregation. But your kinsmen, the whole house of Israel, shall bewail the burning which the Lord has brought about. Leviticus 10:6

This was a clear warning about falsely tearing your clothes and denouncing God. God's wrath would fall upon the people. When the high priest rent his garments in front of Jesus, this was symbolic of two things.

The first was that he was rending his garments to signify the blasphemy he perceived Jesus has spoken. The priest had asked him whether he was the Messiah. Jesus had replied 'I am' The priest did not believe him.

The second symbolic act is that It is traditional that Jews tear their garments when somebody dies and it heralds the seven days of mourning. The high priest tearing his garments baring his naked chest was acknowledging also Jesus as a dead man for his perceived blasphemy.

The Lord showed us that in fact the priest who had not recognised the Royal High Priest before him, had condemned himself to death for not recognising and accepting the true Saviour of the Jews. This act also condemned the Jews to separation from God.

It is not a coincidence that this happened at the Fall. Adam and Eve in sinning, recognised their nakedness, they bared their chests in the same way and condemned themselves to death and earth dying. They did not recognise the sovereignty of God and His message.

These two as full embodiment of God would have been representing King and High Priest.

The Lord told us this morning the High priest's role was to halt the works of the devil and satan his minion. He had singularly failed. We either have Jesus on our right hand or the devil as a choice.

Set thou a wicked man over him: and let Satan stand at his right hand. When he shall be judged, let him be condemned: and let his prayer become sin. Let his days be few; and let another take his office. Psalm 109:6-8 KJV

The high priest renounced his rights by listening to the devil. Caiaphas was replaced shortly after.

The Lord then gave us this verse: *There is neither Jew nor Greek, there is neither slave nor free man, there is neither male nor female; for you are all one in Christ Jesus. And if you belong to Christ, then you are Abraham's descendants, heirs according to promise.* Galatians 3:28-29

The high priest's action had opened the door for all to be saved and not just the Jews.

When we had our sovereign wedding and coronation by The Lord in Heaven last year, He reminded Andrew of the linen He tore off from his robe to bind our hands with. He did it He said to show what God has put together, no man can put asunder. It represents the unity of the Bride and the Bridegroom.

Jesus as the Royal High Priest and King of Kings tore His own garment to bind our hands in marriage and it did not represent death. It represented resurrection and life. He said it represented the hands of God, the blessing of Elohim, the Creator of Heaven and earth. He added 'My power is your power.'

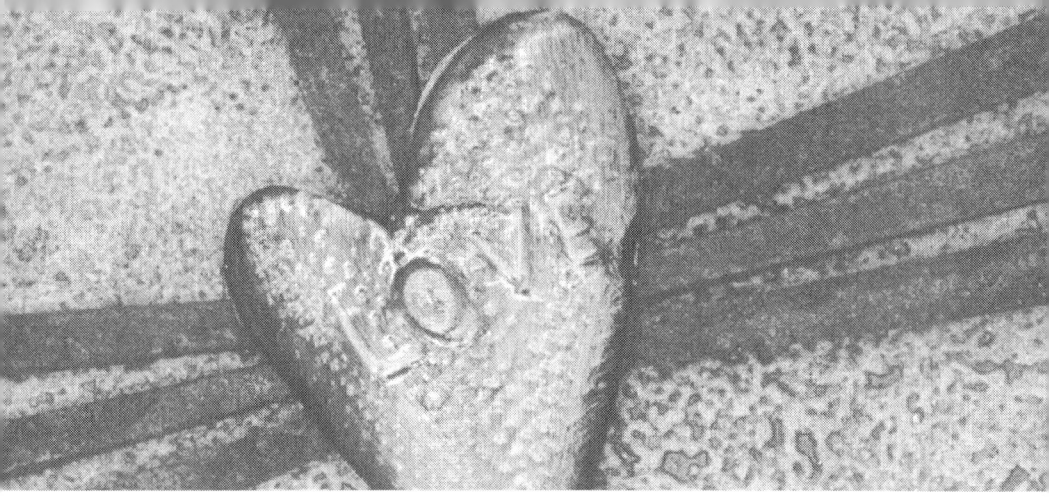

POSTSCRIPT

Time has passed since the first edition was published and of course maturity and more learning has occurred within me.

I have learned to be a son and not an orphan and be expectant of what ever I ask for. I do not petition now. I decree and declare and my faith is based on so many examples of His faithfulness, it is a walk of belief.

Principally my life changed with meeting in 2013 my beloved Elo Ania and becoming one in Christ in a very special way. I had almost given up meeting anyone as I had previously met three beautiful Kingdom ladies over a space of three years. I had fallen in love and proposed with acceptance from all three, not of course at the same time but sequentially. All eventually took fright and decided against marriage.

I had completely disregarded the finer points of a prophecy over me, including a vision I was given, where my future warrior wife would arrive on a black stead in full gear along side me at full gallop and I would not slow down in my purpose on my charger. The Lord told me off when Elo arrived, saying each time I had slowed down and pursued. This was not His instruction. This lesson taught me absolute obedience not lip service obedience.

I have learned that the other side has stolen so much of what Kingdom people should be doing and using. It needs to be taken back by us walking in obedience and then the Lord gives us the gifts; translocation, extra sensory perception, reading people well, discerning the times, telekinesis, speaking to DNA, mind control.

My wife was able, before she was saved, to move matter but she was doing it from the wrong realm. God took away the powers from her and turned her to Him for protection, but slowly He is giving them back for His purpose and not hers.

Many more encounters have happened and healings and ministry and I have acquired a hilarious arsenal of toys the Holy Spirit has given me to help demonstrate His power.

Rather than go back and rewrite the book I have tweaked various areas where the Lord has given me so much more insight and revelation on the Word, coupled with counsel of the Holy Spirit.

One example was about the Pre-Adamic time and Edens location and the fall. Here is the revelation through the scriptures and a great man of God, Paul Keith Davies.

What happened between Creation and the arrival of Adam? The untold story? Between Genesis 1:1 and 1:3 time came into being when Christ came into being. He is the beginning and end, the Aleph and Tav, over billions of years.

I looked on the earth, and behold, there was nothing, and to the sky, and it had no lights. I saw the mountains, and they were trembling, and all the hills were being disturbed. Jeremiah 4:23-26

The strange thing about these verses and the following ones, is that it relates clearly to a period that has nothing to do with the Flood. It is at the beginning of Creation.

In the beginning God made the heaven and the earth. Genesis 1:1

So Jeremiah taken up in the spirit, was shown the cosmos before there was light This means just as the cosmos and time was beginning. And then:

Yet the earth was invisible and unformed, and darkness was over the abyss, and a divine wind was being carried along over the water. Genesis 1:2

God who is perfect, had a creation plan It was never going to be void.

POSTSCRIPT

Thus says the Lord, who made heaven-- this is the God who displayed the earth and made it; he himself marked its limits; he did not make it to be empty but to be inhabited: I am, and there is no other. Isaiah 45:18

And then Jeremiah was shown a world that had had humans, birds, animals and settlements that were all but annihilated. God left something. The Garden? This is the period pre Adam

I looked, and behold, there was no human, and all the birds of the air were being terrified. I saw, and behold, Carmel was a wilderness, and all the cities burned up before the Lord, and before the wrath of his anger they were annihilated. This is what the Lord says: The whole land shall be a wilderness; yet I will not make a full end. Jeremiah 4:25-27

At the time of the revolt by the most beautiful cherub, heylel and the angels were cast into the cosmos and earth. So the prehistoric man and the Mammoths fits with the Bible. The ice age probably happened when the angels were thrown out of Heaven and God decided to blot out the sun and stars. There are billions of years between Genesis 1:1 and Genesis 1:3

Job was shown the same picture.

he who ages mountains, and they do not know it, who overturns them in anger, who shakes what is under heaven from its foundations, and its pillars tremble, who speaks to the sun, and it does not rise, and seals up the stars.. Job 9:5-7

So Genesis 1:3 arrives. The Rebellion or fall of the angels happened before time began. Jesus said He saw the devil fall from eternity, therefore into time, into the Cosmos. Not just earth. Heaven is outside the Cosmos. The fall of Adam happened way later.

The Lord has given us much advice on the power of communion and that we can take it whenever we wish.

INTINCTION

While my beloved and I were taking communion this morning and I was immersing the bread into the Wolfsberry juice, representing His blood. I got zapped by the Holy Spirit majorly. This is and should be a very Holy moment for all. The Lord spoke to me "My blood has to return into the Body. The bread is His body, which is His Church. The wine, which is His blood, is His DNA and His life in us. Our bodies do not function without blood. His blood has to fill the body, the church and us, for it to be alive in Him.

And they continued steadfastly in the apostles' doctrine and fellowship, in the breaking of bread, and in prayers. Acts 2:42 NKJV

As Jesus is water and blood, we must immerse ourselves in the River of Life and His blood.

This is He who came by water and blood - Jesus Christ; not only by water, but by water and blood. And it is the Spirit who bears witness, because the Spirit is truth. 1 John 5:6 NKJV

There is only life in the blood. Without blood flow, there is no life. Without river flow, the earth or ground becomes arid and dies.

The Body of the Church will not function without us being immersed in His Blood. Our bodies will not function either. The Church will not function without regular communion with Him. The Body and the Blood, mixed and immersed together, bring Oneness.

So obvious as to be mind boggling. Us in Oneness individually and corporately creates the living church today.

TIME

He taught us about redeeming time, which sounds quite spooky.

1. Time and the coming of Jesus

The Lord asked us what would be the point of sons of God having no power and authority until He returned for the thousand years. None. He vested in us the title of priest and King.

And has made us kings and priests to His God and Father, to Him be glory and dominion forever and ever. Amen. Revelation 1:6

And have made us kings and priests to our God; And we shall reign on the earth. Revelation 5:10

But you are a chosen generation, a royal priesthood, a holy nation, His own special people, that you may proclaim the praises of Him who called

POSTSCRIPT

you out of darkness into His marvelous light; 1 Peter 2:9

See what happened with Jacob ?

So Jacob served seven years for Rachel, and they seemed only a few days to him because of the love he had for her. Genesis 29:20

So time, with love controlling it, is vastly shortened.

So what is our task as priests and kings among other things? To redeem time. Redeeming time in Greek means 'rescue from loss'. Jesus rescues us from loss. He is our Kinsman Redeemer. We are His vessels in time, to get it back for Him. We can ourselves become kinsmen redeemers. He reminded us of:

"So I will restore to you the years that the swarming locust has eaten, the crawling locust, the consuming locust, and the chewing locust, My great army which I sent among you. Joel 2:25

These four locusts represent natural and spiritual maturity stages, against all the tree of life represents on earth:

- Swarming - eats the fruit
- Crawling - eats the leaves to stop growth
- Consuming - strips the bark and the trees protection
- Chewing - burrows into the heart of the tree to kill it

When we as sons take the seven mountains for the Lord, we are restoring the land back to before time began; pure, cleansed by the Blood and perfect.

For the creation waits in eager expectation for the children of God to be revealed. For the creation was subjected to frustration, not by its own choice, but by the will of the one who subjected it, in hope that the creation itself will be liberated from its bondage to decay and brought into the freedom and glory of the children of God. We know that the whole creation has been groaning as in the pains of childbirth right up to the present time. Not only so, but we ourselves, who have the firstfruits of the Spirit, groan inwardly as we wait eagerly for our adoption to sonship, the redemption of our bodies. Romans 8:19-23

We do the same thing with the lost. ἐξαγοράζω - exagorazō - ex-ag-or-ad'-zo: From G1537 and G59; to buy up, that is, ransom; figuratively to rescue from loss (improve opportunity): - redeem.

The Lord said time is an evil principality to take control over in the spirit. As with all principalities, it is fear based. If people do not understand the principle of eternity, then fear comes in the form of being time bound. Bondage to time.

If we walk in the fullness of His Love, we are able to have control over time as He does. Perfect love casts out all fear! His love never fails. Ergo, our love, if it is like His, will not fail either.

He just said to us "I love spending time with you" and we got so blasted with this message.

Time stands still when one is with Him in the Spirit.

Try soaking and seeing after two physical hours when it felt like ten minutes or five minutes with Him feels like a day.

See then that you walk circumspectly, not as fools but as wise, redeeming the time, because the days are evil. Amen. Ephesians 5:15-16

Time, the name and word is first used in Genesis 4:3.

- Yom means daylight hours and one description of time.
- Chronos means a sequence of events. In Greek mythology, the apparent god of time was Kronos. The Lord told us Kronos was one of the main angels that fell with heylel.
- Kairos means an appointed time or event much like z'mam is in Hebrew.

So we have authority over all these types of time. He put Adam in time where heylel was, but where are we supposed to be seated? In Heavenly places, which is outside time. We can only control time from outside time, in the spirit realm, from eternity and with love.

2. Redeeming the time

You might not believe in transportation or translocation but God does. I was adjusting the grandfather clock that rang once the other evening. But it said 12 o'clock. Very strange.

The Lord told Elo to ask me what was the time on the clock. I called back the time. He said look up 'when the verse says the sun standing still'. This is to do with Israel and us and our ability in the Spirit to the change the course of time.

POSTSCRIPT

Then Joshua spoke to the LORD in the day when the LORD delivered up the Amorites before the sons of Israel, and he said in the sight of Israel, "O sun, stand still at Gibeon, And O moon in the valley of Aijalon." So the sun stood still, and the moon stopped, Until the nation avenged themselves of their enemies. Is it not written in the book of Jashar? And the sun stopped in the middle of the sky and did not hasten to go down for about a whole day. There was no day like that before it or after it, when the LORD listened to the voice of a man; for the LORD fought for Israel.... Joshua 10:12-14

How amazing that Joshua was the only man in the Bible permitted to cause time to stand still.

God wound back time with Hezekiah through Isaiah. Ten degrees is forty minutes. Forty is a key Hebraic number relating for ending the wilderness and entering the promised land. I am sure we will get more revelation on this.

Then Isaiah said, "This is the sign to you from the Lord, that the Lord will do the thing which He has spoken: shall the shadow go forward ten degrees or go backward ten degrees?" And Hezekiah answered, "It is an easy thing for the shadow to go down ten degrees; no, but let the shadow go backward ten degrees." So Isaiah the prophet cried out to the Lord, and He brought the shadow ten degrees backward, by which it had gone down on the sundial of Ahaz. 2 Kings 20:9-11

Jesus said we will do greater things than Him.

See then that you walk circumspectly, not as fools but as wise, redeeming the time, because the days are evil. Ephesians 5:15-16

Philip had his time redeemed too, so he could go on a assignment that was urgent.

When they came up out of the water, the Spirit of the Lord suddenly took Philip away, and the eunuch did not see him again, but went on his way rejoicing. Philip, however, appeared at Azotus and traveled about, preaching the gospel in all the towns until he reached Caesarea. Acts 8:39-40

Look at time from God's perspective - God's physics. Time could to be described as a train that had a front and a back, with carriages in-between defining the years or centuries. God is looking down on this train with us in it. There is an Alef (In the Beginning) and a Bet (an end) from His perspective.

If we, with His permission, are taken out of the train and run along the roof, we are outside time. This is what He did with Philip. People dabbling in the other realm of darkness, are doing this and have been doing it since they were probably first trained by the fallen angels, millennia ago.

As the centuries pass, the marker of time is trundling towards the guards van at the end of the train, like the marker on an old radio moving channels. When we go through the Veil to Heaven, we have to go through this second layer. That is why we must travel in the Blood and not on our own.

Can God slow down time if He wishes? Of course, it is His train. Can He accelerate it for us in an instant to get us somewhere? Yes. He can even speed us at a phenomenal rate outside tim,e while not even disturbing the train's speed.

Just in case you were not aware, time is getting to the very back end of the salvation train!

We, as Sons, are enabled and ennobled to take back time for Him; to slow down matters or intervene to ensure creation stops groaning and decay ends. As decay ends its bondage, creation continues. Age recedes and time continues.

We have brought people into the Kingdom in the most extraordinary circumstances, always guided by Holy Spirit as how to approach and what to say. Here is a fun example:

A HAIR RAISING EXPERIENCE

Well today started off well and continued well. I went to London for meetings and beforehand I passed by my favourite barber, Andreas, a Greek Cypriot and a Kingdom man.

His assistant, Francesca, had had a prophetic word from the Lord via myself four years ago and was still thriving on it.

A new face was there, a lady from the north side of Cyprus. She listened with incredulity to her colleagues story and asked if I was a spiritualist. I told her I was a Holy Spirit man, so she asked if I was a born again Christian. Yep!

So I talked about my walk and testimony and asked if she wanted a demonstration of God's power; of course she did!

I placed my hand above her right hand and released His power. Her arm heated up and fire went round her. She motioned for me to go to the back of the salon, as a client was arriving and Andreas was not ready for me yet. She had felt the living proof. I asked if she wanted to accept Jesus into her heart. Having been brought up as a Muslim, she was not practicing, and her answer was a solid 'Yes'.

She prayed the sinners prayer and God entered her life as she swayed to stay up. I prophesied over her, blessed and gave counsel: contact a friend who was a believer; go to a fellowship, etc. Andreas was going to buy her a bible and her boot-camp was starting today.

Everybody was elated. She felt such peace and lightness.

When God invades the enemy is furious but another soul is won. I deployed angels to protect, minister and train her. Andreas will forget this day nor will Chimi. November 11 marks a new day, new beginnings for her and many. Stand with me to cover and bless her.

I have learned how to approach Muslims, Buddhists and Atheists by talking about the Kingdom and not religion. The Lord has short circuited long discussions on the Bible, by allowing me to demonstrate His awesome power with signs and wonders. People are left with no doubt about the Realm of God and His love for them.

HE IS THE LORD OF THE HOSTS

Here is a note I have inserted on this revelation; Lord of the Hosts, Jesus has been speaking to us of His authority.

Jesus approached and, breaking the silence, said to them, All authority (all power of rule) in heaven and on earth has been given to Me. Matthew 28:18 (AMP)

I walk everyday with Him understanding His authority. Do I fear that the One World Order, the Illuminati and the Anti-Christ will succeed. No way!

Do I fear that freemasonry will take over the world? No!

Do I understand the threats and impact the above are having on our planet? Yes!

Do I think that God cannot and will not deal will them? No!

We are in a spiritual battle not a flesh one. I am supreme in the spirit when I walk with my King. This stuff is mincemeat with the power of my King behind me. He rules outside time. I am dead to time and death and a resurrected being. I am spirit and flesh. If my flesh dies I live on eternally.

This does not mean I avoid these threats and disregard what is going on behind the scenes. I am attached as a warrior to the God of the angel armies. All battle with these principalities of evil running puppets on earth in the seven mountains of influence, I do under His orders and His protection. I do it with love.

Their plans are temporal, based on greed, control and restlessness. My King's plans are based on love, freedom, and peace. There is no place where I would rather be.

TOOLBOX

The weapons we fight with are not the weapons of the world. On the contrary, they have divine power to demolish strongholds.
2 Corinthians 10:4

This is a chapter to 'dip into' and savour. Hopefully it will bring forth fruit. It has no major theme except providing some information that you may find useful in different situations; a variety of tools and knowledge for different tasks.

THE TOOLKIT

This is what makes it so simple. We are not working with our own tools. We are working with God's toolkit. If we were working in our own strength and meagre tools we would get nowhere.[1] Remember, you are armed and protected by the armour.[2]

Study the parts you are given and what they do:
- The Helmet of Salvation
- The Sword of the Spirit and Word
- The Shield of Faith

- The Breastplate of Righteousness
- The Buckle of Truth
- The Sandals of Peace

Remember you will need cover from behind. Wing men, Prayer warrior cover. It is important to note in Ephesians 6, He gives you no back plate to protect you. There is no retreat or turning back. He is behind you covering your back if you need Him.[3]

You carry the Gifts. You carry the seven Spirits. You walk in His authority.[4] Remember you are worthy![5] You are better equipped than a modern day soldier in the earth forces.

A vessel and the Bride needing to be purified.

But the Lord said to him, "Go, for he is a chosen vessel of Mine to bear My name before Gentiles, kings, and the children of Israel. Acts 9:15

REQUIRING PURIFICATION

We need to take up the cross and follow Him.

Then He said to them all, "If anyone desires to come after Me, let him deny himself, and take up his cross daily, and follow Me. For whoever desires to save his life will lose it, but whoever loses his life for My sake will save it. For what profit is it to a man if he gains the whole world, and is himself destroyed or lost? Luke 9:23-25

THE OLD TESTAMENT REQUIREMENT

When Moses had proclaimed every command of the law to all the people, he took the blood of calves, together with water, scarlet wool and branches of hyssop, and sprinkled the scroll and all the people.

He said, "This is the blood of the covenant, which God has commanded you to keep." In the same way, he sprinkled with the blood both the tabernacle and everything used in its ceremonies. In fact, the law requires that nearly everything be cleansed with blood, and without the shedding of blood there is no forgiveness. Hebrews 9:19-22

New covenant replaces old covenant with God.[6] Jesus shed His blood so we could be purified and acceptable.[7] We need to be constantly purified by the Fire of Heaven and the burning heart of Jesus, so that we become refined and pure from the fire. In this way, the Vessel contains God in Us, to then leak to other people. In effect, we are to Host His Presence. We are the vessel or bowl into which Jesus, via the Holy Spirit, pours in the seven spirits.

Why do we do this? It is because we love Him and he adores us. He is our Bridegroom and we are His Bride.

We need to become the Vessel of Honour.[8]

Therefore if anyone cleanses himself from the latter, he will be a vessel for honour, sanctified and useful for the Master, prepared for every good work. 2 Timothy 2:21 NKJV

Read the Book of Esther to understand the significance of who we are in Christ. We are being prepared as royal brides and vessels for His pleasure and love.

THE BRIDE OF CHRIST

I am jealous for you with a godly jealousy. I promised you to one husband, to Christ, so that I might present you as a pure virgin to him. 2 Corinthians 11:2

The Ketubah marriage contract involved both the Jewish man and woman drinking from a cup of wine to seal the contract of marriage. He would not drink of the cup again until they reunited after a year.

Jesus, at the Last Supper was re-enacting this contract to his followers, marrying them to Him in the same way.[9] His marriage contract price was the shedding of His blood.

As women, it is easy to understand being a bride. For men it requires further explanation. This link is a good explanation, drawing on Scripture, from SETUSFREEJESUS

In light of this truth, how can we explain the depth of intimacy with God to that of oneness with the male gender? First, a principal truth in Scripture is that we are neither male nor female in the eyes of God "There is neither Jew nor Greek, slave nor free, male nor female, for you are all one in Christ Jesus"[11]

We established earlier that Adam was both male and female, even as God. Adam was made in the likeness and image of God;

God created man in His own image, in the image of God He created him; male and female He created them Genesis 1:27.

Eve was an external manifestation of the feminine part in Adam. So whether we are male or female we are the external manifestation of God's image and are able to seek a relationship with God as Eve did with Adam and vice versa.

In Hebrew, God's name is the combination of the letters Yud and Hay. The name for Adam is Eish, which is spelled using the Hebrew letters Aleph-Yud-Shin. Eve's name is Elisha, spelled in Hebrew Aleph-Shin-Hay.

The Yud in Adam's name is the male characteristics of God, not found in Eve's name and the Hay in Eve's name is the female characteristics of God not found in Adam's name. Therefore, whether male or female we can have a relationship with Christ in the sense of intimacy, because we are all one in Christ. The "one in Christ" or "he is" is neuter, without regard to gender.

Regardless of our gender we can become one with Christ as preached by Paul.

"Do you not know that he who unites himself with a prostitute is one with her in body? For it is said, The two will become one flesh. But he who unites himself with the Lord is one with him in spirit" 1 Corinthians 6:16-17.

Out of all the servants of God, David is the one of whom it was said: "I have found David the son of Jesse, a man after My heart"[12]

It was not a woman after God's heart, it was a man. Men, you are able to steal the heart of God with your love and passion for Him, just like David. All it takes is a heart devoted to know and love Him[13]

GOD'S IDENTITY

This is especially for people in business.

I believe God is looking for us to identify Him to people on earth. Just as soldiers have uniforms and insignia and regimental colours, He wants us to be identifiable as His soldiers and warriors. However He wants to have a brand. Just like in the business world, He needs a Brand Identifier with a mission statement, strategies, objectives, goals, values and behaviours, alongside a business plan.

Simply put:

God the Father is the mission statement and purpose - Getting to Heaven

God the Son is the Goal and Objectives - we model ourselves on Him

God the Holy Spirit is the means to get there, the planner and the adviser.

The Three cannot be without Each Other, They are integral hence the Trinity. The Son worships the Father. The Spirit worships the Son.

TWENTY BIBLE FACTS ABOUT GOD

These will give you insight into the nature and character of God.

God is eternal (Deuteronomy 33:27; Jeremiah 10:10; Psalm 90:2)

God is infinite (1 Kings 8:22-27; Jeremiah 23:24; Psalm 102:25-27; Revelation 22:13)

God is self-sufficient and self-existent (Exodus 3:13-14; Psalm 50:10-12; Colossians 1:16)

God is omnipresent (present everywhere) (Psalm 139:7-12)

God is omnipotent (all powerful)

God is omniscient (all knowing) (Psalm 139:2-6; Isaiah 40:13-14)

God is unchanging or immutable (Psalm 102:25-27; Hebrews 1:10-12; Hebrews 13:8)

God is sovereign (2 Samuel 7:22; Isaiah 46:9-11)

God is wise (Proverbs 3:19; Romans 16:26-27; 1 Timothy 1:17)

God is holy (Leviticus 19:2; 1 Peter 1:15)

God is righteous and just

God is faithful (Deuteronomy 7:9; Psalm 89:1-8)

God is true and truth (Psalm 31:5; John 14:6; John 17:3; Titus 1:1-2)

God is good (Psalm 25:8; Psalm 34:8; Mark 10:18)

God is merciful (Deuteronomy 4:31; Psalm 103:8-17; Daniel 9:9; Hebrews 2:17)

God is gracious (Exodus 34:6; Psalm 103:8; 1 Peter 5:10)

God is love (John 3:16; Romans 5:8; 1 John 4:8)

God is spirit (John 4:24)

God is light (James 1:17; 1 John 1:5)

God is triune or trinity

Remember He does not control, though He has all authority. He has created an environment where the will of man has a role in the outcome of all matters.

OUR IDENTITY

These are one hundred declarations that will change the way you think about your identity "In Christ" and about "Christ In You"

1. I am faithful (Ephesians 1:1)
2. I am God's child (John 1:12)
3. I have been justified (Romans 5:1)
4. I am Christ's friend (John 15:15)
5. I belong to God (1 Corinthians 6:20)
6. I am a member of Christ's Body (1 Corinthians 12:27)
7. I am assured all things work together for good (Romans 8:28)
8. I have been established, anointed and sealed by God (2 Corinthians 1:21-22)
9. I am confident that God will perfect the work He has begun in me (Philippians 1:6)
10. I am a citizen of heaven (Philippians 3:20)
11. I am hidden with Christ in God (Colossians 3:3)
12. I have not been given a spirit of fear, but of power, love and self-discipline (2 Timothy 1:7)
13. I am born of God and the evil one cannot touch me (1 John 5:18)
14. I am blessed in the heavenly realms with every spiritual blessing (Ephesians 1:3)

15. I am chosen before the creation of the world (Ephesians 1:4, 11)
16. I am holy and blameless (Ephesians 1:4)
17. I am adopted as his child (Ephesians 1:5)
18. I am given God's glorious grace lavishly and without restriction (Ephesians 1:5 & 8)
19. I am in Him (Ephesians 1:7; 1 Corinthians 1:30)
20. I have redemption (Ephesians 1:8)
21. I am forgiven (Ephesians 1:8; Colossians 1:14)
22. I have purpose (Ephesians 1:9 & 3:11)
23. I have hope (Ephesians 1:12)
24. I am included (Ephesians 1:13)
25. I am sealed with the promised Holy Spirit (Ephesians 1:13)
26. I am a saint (Ephesians 1:18)
27. I am salt and light of the earth (Matthew 5:13-14)
28. I have been chosen and God desires me to bear fruit (John 15:1 & 5)
29. I am a personal witness of Jesus Christ (Acts 1:8)
30. I am God's co-worker (2 Corinthians 6:1)
31. I am a minister of reconciliation (2 Corinthians 5:17-20)
32. I am alive with Christ (Ephesians 2:5)
33. I am raised up with Christ (Ephesians 2:6;Colossians 2:12)
34. I am seated with Christ in the heavenly realms (Ephesians 2:6)
35. I have been shown the incomparable riches of God's grace (Ephesians 2:7)
36. God has expressed His kindness to me (Ephesians 2:7)
37. I am God's workmanship (Ephesians 2:10)
38. I have been brought near to God through Christ's blood (Ephesians 2:13)
39. I have peace (Ephesians 2:14)
40. I have access to the Father (Ephesians 2:18)
41. I am a member of God's household (Ephesians 2:19)
42. I am secure (Ephesians 2:20)
43. I am a holy temple (Ephesians 2:21; 1 Corinthians 6:19)
44. I am a dwelling for the Holy Spirit (Ephesians 2:22)

45. I share in the promise of Christ Jesus (Ephesians 3:6)
46. God's power works through me (Ephesians 3:7)
47. I can approach God with freedom and confidence (Ephesians 3:12)
48. I know there is a purpose for my sufferings (Ephesians 3:13)
49. I can grasp how wide, long, high and deep Christ's love is (Ephesians 3:18)
50. I am completed by God (Ephesians 3:19)
51. I can bring glory to God (Ephesians 3:21)
52. I have been called (Ephesians 4:1; 2 Timothy 1:9)
53. I can be humble, gentle, patient and lovingly tolerant of others (Ephesians 4:2)
54. I can mature spiritually (Ephesians 4:15)
55. I can be certain of God's truths and the lifestyle which He has called me to (Ephesians 4:17)
56. I can have a new attitude and a new lifestyle (Ephesians 4:21-32)
57. I can be kind and compassionate to others (Ephesians 4:32)
58. I can forgive others (Ephesians 4:32)
59. I am a light to others, and can exhibit goodness, righteousness and truth (Ephesians 5:8-9)
60. I can understand what God's will is (Ephesians 5:17)
61. I can give thanks for everything (Ephesians 5:20)
62. I do not have to always have my own agenda (Ephesians 5:21)
63. I can honour God through marriage (Ephesians 5:22-33)
64. I can parent my children with composure (Ephesians 6:4)
65. I can be strong (Ephesians 6:10)
66. I have God's power (Ephesians 6:10)
67. I can stand firm in the day of evil (Ephesians 6:13)
68. I am dead to sin (Romans 1:12)
69. I am not alone (Hebrews 13:5)
70. I am growing (Colossians 2:7)
71. I am His disciple (John 13:15)
72. I am prayed for by Jesus Christ (John 17:20-23)
73. I am united with other believers (John 17:20-23)

74. I am not in want (Philippians 4:19)
75. I possess the mind of Christ (1 Corinthians 2:16)
76. I am promised eternal life (John 6:47)
77. I am promised a full life (John 10:10)
78. I am victorious (1 John 5:4)
79. My heart and mind is protected with God's peace (Philippians 4:7)
80. I am chosen and dearly loved (Colossians 3:12)
81. I am blameless (1 Corinthians 1:8)
82. I am set free (Romans 8:2; John 8:32)
83. I am crucified with Christ (Galatians 2:20)
84. I am a light in the world (Matthew 5:14)
85. I am more than a conqueror (Romans 8:37)
86. I am the righteousness of God (2 Corinthians 5:21)
87. I am safe (1 John 5:18)
88. I am part of God's kingdom (Revelation 1:6)
89. I am healed from sin (1 Peter 2:24)
90. I am no longer condemned (Romans 8:1, 2)
91. I am not helpless (Philippians 4:13)
92. I am overcoming (1 John 4:4)
93. I am persevering (Philippians 3:14)
94. I am protected (John 10:28)
95. I am born again (1 Peter 1:23)
96. I am a new creation (2 Corinthians 5:17)
97. I am delivered (Colossians 1:13)
98. I am redeemed from the curse of the Law (Galatians 3:13)
99. I am qualified to share in His inheritance (Colossians 1:12)
100. I am victorious (1 Corinthians 15:57)

THE SEVEN SPIRITS OF GOD

The seven lamps that are the Spirits before the Throne. Revelation 4:4

The Spirit of the Lrd will rest on him - the Spirit of wisdom and of understanding, the Spirit of counsel and of might, the Spirit of the knowledge and fear of the Lord. Isaiah 11:2

Genesis 9:12-15 tells us of the rainbow covenant between God and man. The colours follow the seven spirits.

1. the Spirit of the Lord: Red
2. the Spirit of wisdom: Orange
3. the Spirit of understanding: Yellow
4. the Spirit of counsel: Green
5. the Spirit of might: Blue
6. the Spirit of knowledge: Indigo
7. and the Spirit of the fear of the Lord: Violet

One gift you may receive is to see colours in the Holy Spirit world. This will help to see the heavenly aura around a person and what gifts have been bestowed on them so far.

Ian Clayton has some marvellous teaching on this on his website: www.sonofthunder.org

THE REDEMPTIVE GIFTS

There are seven gifts listed in the Romans 12:6-8:

- Prophet
- Servant
- Teacher
- Exhorter/ Encourager
- Giver
- Ruler
- Mercy

I read the following interpretations on these by an Anonymous writer. Do you relate to any of these?

PROPHET: Moody. Articulate. Passionate. Generous. Intense. A keen sense of justice and righteousness. Loves the underdog. Ideologically driven. Creative. Judgmental. Extreme.

The redemptive gift of Prophet is very different from the gift of prophesying. While prophets understand the future through revelation, those with the redemptive gift of Prophet understand the future through the use of Biblical principles.

SERVANT: Diligent. No enemies. Joyous. Helpful. Alert. Hospitable. High spiritual authority. Low self-image. Impeccably honest. Team player. Prone to the 'victim spirit'.

God gives the redemptive gift of Service the highest level of spiritual authority because they can be trusted to use it for the Kingdom instead of for themselves. However, until the Servant sees himself as God sees him, that gift of spiritual authority remains underutilised.

TEACHER: Need to validate truth. Processes slowly. Deep family loyalty. Sees the big picture. Sense of humour. High authority over predator spirit.

Intimacy is a major birthright of the Teacher. When the teacher focuses on doctrine rather than on Father, it leaves the church losing.

EXHORTER: People person. Obsessive compulsive. Verbally expressive. High energy. In motion. Loves change. Dramatic. Melodramatic. Superb teacher. Natural leader. Fun. Late. Real late.

While the Exhorter is the most spontaneously relational of all the gifts, his real strength is revealing the nature of God. The Exhorter has an unparalleled ability to see God in Scripture and to cause us to see our world differently because we have a bigger perspective of God.

GIVER: Private. Intuitive. Insightful. Cautious. Chameleon. Good listener. Very independent. Impulsive. Stable. Contradictory. Frugal. Unpredictable. Multifaceted. Devoid of shame. Family focused.

The gift of Giving has the amazing ability to adapt to almost any situation without being changed at all. While they seem to fit in well, they typically retain all their core values rather than embrace the values of the community around them.

RULER: Busy. Real busy. Thinks big. On time. Reliable. Leader. Fearless. Not easily swayed. Visionary. Team builder. Multi-tasks easily. Reads people well.

The Ruler has the highest ability to get maximum effectiveness out of a 'poor labour pool'. God has graced them with a combination of love and wisdom that enables the mature Ruler to accomplish extraordinary things with a team that appears to be highly inadequate.

MERCY: Intuitive. Intuitive. Intuitive. Safe. Sensitive. Loves beauty. Defines the ambiance. No enemies. Works hard. Hugely compliant. Stubborn in the nicest sort of way.

The gift of Mercy is dramatically different than the previous six gifts. The Mercy hears God with his/her heart while the others tend to hear God with their mind. God uses the gift of Mercy to bring the spiritual climate into right alignment through the blessing of Presence.

Some views on the enemy's plan and how to unmask them.

Recommended reading on the web:

www.scmgrasshopper.com/RedemptiveGifts.pdf

www.theslg.com/SearchResults.asp?Cat=79

Redemptive gift of England series by Arthur Burk.

THE FOUR LIVING CREATURES

and in front of the throne there is something like a sea of glass, like crystal. Around the throne, and on each side of the throne, are four living creatures, full of eyes in front and behind: the first living creature like a lion, the second living creature like an ox, the third living creature with a face like a human face, and the fourth living creature like a flying eagle. And the four living creatures, each of them with six wings, are full of eyes all around and inside. Day and night without ceasing they sing, 'Holy, holy, holy, the Lord God the Almighty, who was and is and is to come.' And whenever the living creatures give glory and honour and thanks to the one who is seated on the throne, who lives for ever and ever, the twenty-four elders fall before the one who is seated on the throne and worship the one who lives for ever and ever; they cast their crowns before the throne, singing. Revelation 4:6-10

The four attributes of God full of eyes seeing into eternity, past and future, forward and backward. This is not the God of 'whoops' as Bobby Conner quoted. He makes no mistakes. He is Sovereign.

OIL, GRAIN AND WINE

He will love you, bless you, and multiply you. He will also bless the fruit of your womb and the fruit of your ground, your grain and your wine and your oil, the increase of your herds and the young of your flock, in the land that he swore to your fathers to give you. You shall be blessed above all peoples. There shall not be male or female barren among you or among your livestock. And the Lord will take away from you all sickness, and none of the evil diseases of Egypt, which you knew, will he inflict on you, but he will lay them on all who hate you. Deuteronomy 7:13-15

Oil is for healing and anointing and protection. This is tremendously powerful. Wine is for the `Joy of the Lord'. Bread is sourced from grain and is the food of life. Jesus said "I am the bread of Life". The bread and wine symbolise communion.

EXPOSING LIES OF THE ENEMY

When you expose a lie that you or others have associated with the Godhead, due to equating to something that has happened on earth:

1. Forgive the person.
2. Renounce and break agreement with the lie.
3. Nail it to the cross.
4. Hand it to Jesus.
5. Ask what Jesus has in exchange for the person: The truth.
6. Ask the Godhead what they think of the person.

For example:

A cruel birth father that causes one to feel our Father in heaven is like the earthly one.

A cursing peer or sibling who makes one feel Jesus is like that.

An unloving mother who makes one feel that the Holy Spirit is like that.

DISCIPLESHIP TRAINING

As you go out you will be asked to guide and teach. I have included Ian McCormack's own list of guidelines which I feel is really anointed. It gives all the references needed.

Discipleship Key - KNOW JESUS as your PERSONAL LORD & SAVIOUR. {John 17:3}{Romans 10:8-13}

To then get committed into a local church/body of believers. {Hebrews 10:23-25} {1 Corinthians 12:12-27}

Become a Disciple of Jesus. {Matthew 28:18-20}

Take up your cross & follow Him. {Matthew 16:24}

Discipleship Basics

Repent of all your sins {Acts 2:38}

Ask the Lord Jesus Christ to cleanse you of all your sins with His precious blood {1 John 1:5-7}{Ephesians 5:1-16}

Love God with all your heart & your neighbour as yourself {Mark 12:29-31}

Daily Read the Bible: Man shall not live by bread alone but by every word that proceeds out of the mouth of God {Matthew 4:4}

Worship: {Ephesians 5:18-21}{Philippians 3:3}{Revelation 4:10}

Baptism in Water: {Act 2:38-41}{Acts 10:44-48}{Acts 16:30-33}{Acts 19:1-5}

Baptism in the Holy Spirit: {Acts 2:1-4}{Acts 2:38-39}{Acts 10:40-46}{Acts 19:6}{1 Corinthians 14:1-5}

Communion: {Acts 2:46-47}{1 Corinthians 11:20-34}

Prayer: {Ephesians 6:18-19}{Colossians 4:2}{Luke 6:12}

Tithing: {Deuteronomy 14:22}{Malachi 3:8-11}{Mark 12:43}

Fellowship: {Acts 2:46-47}{1 John 1:7}

Fasting: {Luke 2:37}{Acts 14: 23}

Spiritual Warfare: {Ephesians 6:10-18}{2 Corinthians 10:3-6}{1 John 4:1-6}

LIVE THE FRUITS OF THE SPIRIT

But the fruit of the Spirit is love, joy, peace, forbearance, kindness, goodness, faithfulness, gentleness and self-control. Against such things there is no law. Galatians 5:22-23

ANGELS AND POWER TO COMMAND

I have subsequently learned that the Lord does actually deploy angels to His sons. I cannot tell you on what criterior but I have been given permission to command various types of angels and send them forth for His purposes. It is a sort of delegation of power and I always ask permission first. One person was on messaging with me in New Zealand was in dire need of angelic protection. In an instant after I sent a platoon of warrior angels, her room was filled with powerful angels awaiting orders!

A DIFFERENT CALENDAR

Many Christians today link themselves to the Jewish calendar and activities under the Hebraic timetable and feasts. We are from the tribes of Israel and Jesus was a Jew. We need to understand our heritage. The Chinese, Jewish and Muslim calendar starts 5775 years ago. Each new year starts at Rosh Hashana in September.

Jewish calendar, Tishrei Yom Tov:
5775 (2014-2015) = Year of Ox
5776 (2015-2016) = Year of the Lion
5777 (2016-2017) = Year of the Man
5778 (2017-2018) = Year of Eagle

OTHER KEY TOOLS

    Activation and authority - the Davidian Keys:
    Isaiah 22:22 - Opening and closing doors
    Matthew 16:19 - Binding and loosing

    The following are things to do and pratice
        Pray.

Be a Vessel.

Be Royal.

Dance.

Praise.

Worship.

Give thanks.

Music.

Banners.

Prophetic Art.

Anointing with Oils.

Words of Knowledge,

Listening Prayer.

Deliverance and Ministry.

Fasting.

Soaking in the Presence.

Flying in the Spirit.

Supernatural Downloads for strategy.

School and Study.

THE BIBLE - quoting.

Use of the Spirit and Word - the double-edged sword.

Give Testimonies.

Prayer warriors for cover.

Intercession.

Take Communion regularly. This is very important. Christ comes to reside in us and empower us. He is 'the Bread of life' and Manna from Heaven. His blood and body allow us to manifest His power.

WARRIOR'S QUIVER
INTRODUCTION

"Very truly I tell you, whoever believes in me will do the works I have been doing, and they will do even greater things than these, because I am going to the Father. And I will do whatever you ask in my name, so that the Father may be glorified in the Son. You may ask me for anything in my name, and I will do it" John 14:12-14

Earth was intended to follow the blueprint of Heaven.

Following the first publishing of this book in June 2012, the Lord started to nudge me on another book. Then two people prophesied over me. They said another book was on the way and I would receive downloads from Him.

It was clear from inception this was going to be all revelatory. There would be some teaching but the bulk would be matters He would be explaining to me for dissemination to the World.

He took me first back to the Lord's Prayer or better described as the Apostles' Prayer. He kept on repeating "On Earth as it is in Heaven...." to me like a mantra so I would ingest and digest it. This is the strap line of the book.

This is Father's Kingdom as the prayer is addressed to God the Father.

Kingdom means King's Domain (a territory, state, people or community ruled or reigned over by a king or queen; the eternal Sovereignty of God).

If our task is to bring His Kingdom to Earth that is fine[1]. What He was reminding me is that everything originated in Heaven.[2] If we are thought of before time began by the Uncreated One, nothing on Earth as it stands is original. It all started in Heaven.[2] By looking at things from a Heavenly perspective we can understand more clearly why human thought and processes have developed the way they do.

Sometimes it has taken years and years for things to become apparent and the revelation of its simplicity shines through. God makes nothing complicated. Everything He has planned and worked is perfect, efficient and purposeful. He is the Author and Finisher.[3] We are part of the assembly line on earth, chapter two, paragraph three, for example.

He has taught me this revelation about signs, and wonders, healings, and miracles. I do not need to know His plans. He just unfolds to me what I need to know when I need to know it and through obedience and intimacy I do what I am told. His timing is perfect. Mine is faulty. He may bring healing to someone at a far slower speed than I would wish. He may delay a miracle. He works outside time with His angels.

One of Man's challenges and errors is that as he has progressively detached himself from the Godhead. He is striving, examining and learning in his own strength, not God's. This has been a major mistake.[4]

"For my thoughts are not your thoughts, neither are your ways my ways," declares the Lord. As the heavens are higher than the earth, so are my ways higher than your ways and my thoughts than your thoughts." Isaiah 55:8-9

I believe He is bringing in a new breed of men and women who listen to Him closely and learn heavenly things that have never been revealed before.[5] These people have attained sonship and spend much time with Papa God, Jesus and the Holy Spirit. They have an intimacy and friendship unattainable on earth. They hunger for Him and lean on Him for advice and revelation.

These people are in all spheres of the world and scattered around the Seven Mountains of influence.

- Family
- Education
- Government
- Religion
- Economy
- Celebration
- Media

Because they are trusted and obedient, they become open to revelations and mystical experiences, which allow them to see how Heaven is run and how the Godhead works. Love pervades all in Heaven, as it should do on earth. The latter starts to fade even with a flicker of a match.[6]

Those of you who have tasted heaven will know what I mean. It is indescribable, all embracing and one never wants to return to earth. No epithet, aphorism, or adjective can describe God's unconditional love for us. Since He loved us first, we learn to love Him.[7]

It would be impossible otherwise. When we start to love Him then we learn to release His love through us to others.[8]

It does not stop here. He wants to instruct us and educate us in His ways.[9]

This book is about that type of instruction. How we can receive instructions and use them for His Purpose.

I think we are entering a new phase in end times where the full force and authority of the King of Kings is unleashed against the devilish remnant on earth and in the heavenlies. He is beginning to use humans in a way far beyond their ken to take down the principalities and controls of the devil over the seven mountains of influence, countries, cities, and towns. He is starting to reveal the truths of His Kingdom that all emanated from Heaven in the first place.

Warriors of Love is a type of primer, similar to school primers on Latin and Greek. It is a foundational tool for people to understand the importance of God's end time army and why we need to join it. The structure I now realise that he gave me, models our earthly armies. 'As it is in Heaven.' What a surprise!

The revelation of the sequel to Warriors is just becoming apparent now to me. I was already acknowledging to myself that everything did originate in Heaven.

For some time now He has given me the gift of seeing angels but particularly worship angels. Why I wondered? My task was to introduce them to their earthy mortals who were musicians and worship leaders.[10] This I have done obediently and with much hilarity and success. I will recount two cases later. The message He was giving me was that all inspiration and music that glorifies Him came from Heaven in the first place. I am sure you can begin to see this. Where there is Heaven impacting earth, the devil has always tried to counterfeit and change this.[11] Offshoots appear that are not Godly. All sounds and words come from heaven. Worship angels guide and download to musicians and songwriters inspired music and libretti for glorification of their Maker.[12] How amazing is that?

As The Lord started to unpack the need for another book, He kept on giving me the words 'a Quiver of Arrows.' I realised as a warrior it was one of my weapons. I have been given many prophetic words long before I wrote Warriors, that I was a warrior and that I was an archer in the spirit.

What was so special about this particular weapon instead of a sword or dagger or spear? Then it came out. 'I am the Quiver, you are the arrows!' This completely 'blitzed' me for a few days as I talked it through with my prayer partner Brian Trueman.

Well, a quiver is a vessel and yes, we use it to put arrows in. When He left earth to re-join His Father, Jesus left the other part of the Godhead to remain to guide counsel and protect us on earth: the Holy Spirit.

Quiver also means as a verb: To shake with a slight, rapid, tremulous movement; to vibrate, and often with emotion. Does this begin to sound like the Holy Spirit? Yes.

If Jesus is the quiver via the Holy Spirit and we are His arrows, suddenly our purpose becomes clear. He fires us out into the world. We are safe inside the quiver protected and ready for action.

Then He said "My warriors carry the Quiver (Me) and fire out my arrows at people!" So not only are we His arrows but we are obviously sending something out on the arrows that is not of us but of Him. This makes sense.

A picture was given to a beloved sister of mine, who had no knowledge of the book, or of the title, or the revelation I had received on arrows.

'While we were soaking at Prayer School today I had a picture of the Lord with a quiver and He was somehow carrying lots of different substances around him. He took arrows one by one from His quiver and dipped each one in a particular substance, then fired it at each one of us, so that we each received from him whatever we needed today. That was my impression of what he was doing. There was an impression of thoughtful purpose, but He was half smiling too!'

Well that was a good confirmation for me. Then came the blockbuster. He is the God of ambushes. That is why I adore Him.

I was 'Googling' a 'quiver full of arrows' and kept on alighting on Mr J Archer's book "No enlightenment"

Then, tucked below I saw the verse Psalm 127:4-5 listed briefly.

Now while I was absorbing these passages, my iPhone is playing music in my left ear. Out of one hundred and twenty one songs of soaking music and numerous stanzas, guess what was being sung? You guessed it: Psalm 127:4-4 by the Sons of Korah! I opened up my bible and read it:

Like arrows in the hands of a warrior so are the children of one's youth. How blessed is the man whose quiver is full of them; They will not be ashamed when they speak with their enemies in the gate. (NASB)

I just burst into paroxysms of laughter and giggling. I reckon they were chuckling in Heaven too.

Coincidence the cynic would say? No, God Incidence. There is no such thing as coincidence.[13]

I was pretty convinced I was on the right track but the Lord gave me a final confirmation at a weeks teaching event a few days later, run by Holy Trinity Brompton (HTB). One of their last speakers, Jenetzen Franklin, spoke on gatekeepers and archers and then launched into Psalm 127:4-5 and even took out a toy bow to demonstrate the purpose.

Having received the revelation and the extraordinary confirmations I started to proceed to writing.

The next revelation to arrive before I was even given a break, was that the fact that the book was the quiver and the chapters were the arrows! This seemed pretty logical if the arrows were the revelations He wanted to share. As He was firing arrows at us in the Prayer School, revelations hit us all individually specifically targeted for each of us.

So what was He dipping the arrowheads into and what was the relevance in Psalm 127 to the simile of children?

Jenetzen Franklin said the children were our arrows we fired into the future bridging the generations. I think he was 'spot on.' As advanced believers we need to guide and encourage children in the faith, to be nurtured properly so they like us become the arrows being fired.

We are firing Heavenly arrows that represent the true blueprint from Heaven, and not the false one. This may cover values and behaviours, dealing in the truth, and how to interact with people. Similarly in the five-fold ministries which we are supposed to carry, all the correct values of behaviours should manifest in each gift we are using. This is "on earth as it is in heaven." A consistent approach that can be measured in the whole of our lifestyle, that demonstrates grace, holiness, humility, love, and compassion.

In God's world, things can take on multiple facets and applications.[14] In Warriors, I refer to the revelation of what sunflowers mean to Him. What 'surfing the spirit' means. It was quickly becoming apparent he had a torrent of comparisons to give me that showed how everything started in Heaven and how we could relate back earthly things to Heaven and gain wisdom and understanding from the conclusions.

As the warrior archers for the Lord climbed the mountain to avoid the hordes of demonised people, they fired arrows with purpose from various heights. Some hit their mark and sometimes they had no effect on wounding or terminating the enemy. Some were directed at the devil's own people and many at the captive Christians who had demons on them.

Clearly the choice of arrows was very relevant and at some heights and trajectories, the contents on the end of the arrow tip had greater impact. Why? Each arrow had a different impact and success. The wrong choice produced the wrong impact..... Onwards to Arrow One!

BOOKLIST

Below are some of Andrew's suggested Warrior books to read:
- All his books - Bill Johnson
- Like a Mighty Wind - Mel Tari
- Culture of Honor - Danny Silk
- A Glimpse of Eternity - Ian McCormack
- Angels on Assignment - Roland Buck
- Lost Art of Intercession - James Goll
- God on Mute & Red Moon Rising - Pete Greig
- Miraculous Love - Maggie Colvin
- Unlocking Heaven & Ultimate Treasure Hunt - Kevin Dedmon
- What's so Amazing about Grace - Philip Yancy
- The Grace Outpouring – Roy Godwin
- All his books – Kris Valloton
- Open my Eyes Lord- Gary Oates
- The Purpose Driven Life – Rick Warren
- God's Generals series - Roberts Liardon
- All his books – Jerame Nelson
- The Final Quest, the Call, & Torch and the Sword - Rick Joyner
- Faith the Link with God's power – Reinhard Bonnke
- As in the Days of Noah - David Powell with Paul Keith Davis

Pursuit of the Holy - Corey Russell

Ekklesia Rising - Liz Wright

Forgiveness - Frank Damazio

Justice of God and Shepherd's Rod - Bobby Conner

God is a Match Maker – Derek Prince

All his books - CS Lewis

Seven Mountain Prophecy and Mantle- Johnny Enlow

The Bible of course

END-NOTES

Introduction
1. Jeremiah 29:11
2. 1 Corinthians 13:8
3. 1 John 4:8
4. 1 Corinthians 13:4-8
5. 1 Timothy 6:15
6. Revelation 5:10
7. Revelation 4:11
8. Isaiah 61:1-7
9. Psalms 86:15, 2 Timothy 2:13 AMP
10. John 15:5 AMP
11. Romans 2:4 AMP
12. 1 John 4:19
13. Philippians 1:6
14. Romans 6:18
15. 1 Timothy 3:5
16. John 10:10, Proverbs 6:31; Psalms 79:12
17. Proverbs 5:1 AMP
18. Colossians 1:15

19. Psalms 130:4
20. John 5:41
21. Ephesians 1:6
22. John 8:32
23. 2 Timothy 1:7
24. Galatians 5:6
25. Galatians 3:28
26. Revelation 12:11
27. Romans 6:4-5
28. John 3:16
29. Psalms 90:4
30. Psalms 104:4
31. Psalms 103:20
32. Job 22:28
33. Psalms 91:11
34. Luke 15:7-10
35. 1 Corinthians 13:2
36. Matthew 25:23
37. Romans 8:14

Chapter 2 - Paradise Regained
1. Matthew 10:41
2. Exodus 20:4-5

Chapter 3 - Why Enter God's Army
1. Psalm 84:1
2. Acts 4:13
3. 1 Corinthians 15:55
4. Matthew 10:16
5. Isaiah 14:13
6. Revelation 12:4
7. Genesis 6:2
8. Matthew 28:18

9. Romans 6:6
10. Ephesians 1:21, Hebrews 4:3, Ecclesiastes 3:1-11
11. Ephesians 6:10
12. Colossians 1:19-20
13. Jeremiah 1:7
14. Hebrews 10:17
15. 1 John 2:27
16. Matthew 23:12
17. Ephesians 5:11, Matthew 8:23-27
18. Numbers 12:8
19. Proverbs 25:2

Chapter 4 - Basic Qualifications
1. 1 Corinthians 1:27
2. 2 Corinthians 12:9-10
3. John 15:5
4. 1 Corinthians 2:4, 1 Corinthians 4:20
5. Colossians 1:15
6. Matthew 5:15-17
7. Romans 6:4, Ephesians 5:26, 1 Peter 3:21, John 3:3-8
8. 1 Corinthians 15:55-57 NLT
9. John 1:12, Acts 1:8
10. Ephesians 1:6, 1 John 4:17
11. Philippians 2:7-8
12. Jeremiah 33:3

Chapter 5 - Opposition
1. Matthew 6:22, Hebrews 12:2 AMP
2. Revelation 12:11
3. John 8:36
4. Ephesians 5:1 NASB
5. John 19:30
6. 1 John 5:4, Ephesians 2:8

7. Philippians 2:9-10
8. John 10:10
9. Ephesians 6:17
10. James 4:6-7
11. Esther 7:9-10
12. Proverbs 6:31

Chapter 6 - Bootcamp
1. Micah 6:8
2. Psalms 144:1
3. 2 Timothy 1:7
4. Proverbs 29:23
5. Proverbs 5:1 AMP; Proverbs 3:11-12
6. Proverbs 4:23
7. John 10:10; Galatians 5:22
8. 1 John 4:19
9. Psalms 19:5; John 3:29
10. Philippians 2:13
11. Ecclesiastes 4:9-10
12. Luke 22:31-32
13. 1 John 2:27
14. Deuteronomy 7:9
15. Mark 16:18
16. Proverbs 5:1 AMP
17. Proverbs 15:1
18. Psalms 150:6
19. 1 Corinthians 10:31
20. John 4:23, 2 Chronicles 16:9
21. Psalms 29:2; Psalms 95:6-7
22. Revelation 4:10; Revelation 5:11-14; Revelation 19:1-7 & 10
23. Jeremiah 1:5
24. 1 Samuel 16:7; Exodus 34:14
25. Matthew 18:2-4

26. Genesis 1:26-27
27. Matthew 6:7
28. Isaiah 65:24
29. Proverbs 3:5; Isaiah 55:6-8
30. 1 Thessalonians 5:21; 1 John 4:1-6
31. Matthews 1:20
32. 2 Corinthians 4:18
33. 1 John 4:1
34. Matthew 20:28
35. Luke 6:42
36. Job 23:2
37. Isaiah 28:11-12
38. John 5:41 AMP
39. Psalms 119:66
40. Romans 10:9; John 14:6
41. 2 Thessalonians 2:9
42. 2 Corinthians 11:14
43. 1 John 4:8; Galatians 5:6

Chapter 7 - Regular Army
1. John 8:36
2. 2 Timothy 1:7
3. Matthew 14:29
4. Matthew 23:12
5. John 15:5
6. John 3:27
7. 1 Corinthians 7:32-34

Chapter 8 - The Front Line
1. 1 Peter 5:8
2. Isaiah 62:6
3. Galatians 5:25
4. Zephaniah 3:17

5. Proverbs 19:20
6. 1 Corinthians 12:8 NIV
7. Ecclesiastes 9:16-18
8. Proverbs 12:26
9. Hebrews 1:14 AMP
10. Romans 8:34
11. 1 John 1:5
12. Philippians 1:6
13. Psalms 147:3
14. Romans 8:15; Galatians 4:16
15. 1 Peter 2:9; John 18:36
16. Revelation 19:16
17. Matthew 5:8, 20
18. 2 Corinthians 4:7
19. Proverbs 29:25
20. Matthew 23:26
21. 1 Peter 2:13-14; Romans 13:1-7
22. Philippians 2:13; Colossians 1:27
23. John 15:5
24. 1 Corinthians 14:1; Romans 12:6; Jeremiah 1:5
25. John 4:6; John 4:31-34
26. 1 Corinthians 14:13
27. Ephesians 4:3
28. 2 Corinthians 4:18
29. Ephesians 2:20
30. James 1:22-25

Chapter 9 - Special Forces
1. 1 Timothy 4:8
2. Revelation 12:11
3. Ephesians 4:27
4. 2 Corinthians 6:14
5. 1 John 1:5; Psalms 139:12 NLV

6. Psalms 130:20
7. Psalms 91:11-16
8. Matthew 10:16
9. Jeremiah 9:4
10. Matthew 7:15
11. Deuteronomy 32:20
12. Deuteronomy 11:24
13. Romans 8:19-23
14. Job 22:28; Esther 7:1-4
15. 2 Chronicles 7:14
16. James 5:17-18
17. Isaiah 46:10 AMP
18. Jeremiah 29:11; Romans 8:28
19. 1 Chronicles 12:32
20. 1 Thesselonians 5:20-21; 1 John 4:1; 2 Corinthians 13:1
21. Luke 19:10
22. Psalms 115:16; John 3:3-8; John 18:36
23. 1 Corinthians 12:3; John 14:6
24. Leviticus 18:21
25. Revelation 19:11
26. Hebrews 13:8; Romans 11:11-31
27. Galatians 5:22-23
28. Galatians 5:14; Matthew 5:17
29. Hebrews 10:1-18
30. 1 Corinthians 13:4-8
31. 1 John 2:15
32. Luke 10:19; Colossians 2:15
33. Matthew 12:43-45
34. http://www.riversoflife.net/ministry/freedom.html
35. http://www.theophostic.com/
36. http://www.jesusministries.org/
37. John 15:5
38. Romans 12:14

Chapter 10 - Lessons Learnt
1. John 19:30
2. Hebrews 12:2 NKJV
3. Ecclesiastes 3:1
4. Matthew 6:10
5. Genesis 21:2; Genesis 17:17
6. Proverbs 25:11 HCS
7. Psalms 16:11
8. Matthew 8:5-10
9. Luke 3:22 NIV
10. Job 22:28
11. Colossians 1:27

Chapter 14 - Toolbox
1. 2 Corinthians 12:9
2. Ephesians 6: 13-17
3. Isaiah 52:12
4. Matthew 28:18-20
5. Matthew 10:29-31
6. Hebrews 8:13
7. Hebrews 9:13-14
8. 2 Timothy 2:21
9. Matthew 27:27-28
10.
11.
12. 1 Samuel 13:12
13. 1 Kings 8:61

Chapter 15 - Warriors Quiver
1. Matthew 3:12
2. Colossians 1:16
3. Hebrews 12:2
4. Ephesians 6:10

ENDNOTES

5. Matthew 11:25
6. 2 Corinthians 6:14
7. 1 John 4:19
8. Philippians 4:13
9. Psalms 32:8
10. Psalms 91:11
11. 2 Corinthians 11:14
12. Luke 6:45
13. Proverbs 16:33
14. 1 Corinthians 15:46

Printed in Poland
by Amazon Fulfillment
Poland Sp. z o.o., Wrocław